UNKNOWN HORIZONS

Unknown Horizons

by

CJ Birch

2017

UNKNOWN HORIZONS

ISBN 13: 978-1-62639-938-9

This Trade Paperback Original Is Published By
Bold Strokes Books, Inc.
P.O. Box 249
Valley Falls, NY 12185

First Edition: April 2017

Credits
Editor: Katia Noyes
Production Design: Stacia Seaman
Cover Design: W.E. Percival

Acknowledgments

There are so many minds that go into creating a book, and this book wouldn't exist without a lot of amazing minds! Thanks to all the early readers, especially those on Wattpad who pointed out some very basic flaws in my science and gave me the encouragement to keep going. I've tried to keep the science in this book as accurate as possible, although in some cases I may have taken a turn more toward fiction than science.

Also, so many thanks to Katia Noyes, my editor, for always asking the right questions, for always knowing what was lacking and where, and for teaching me that commas are important and I should use more of them. This book wouldn't be even half as good without you.

Thanks to my mom for never once telling me that my dreams were silly.

Thanks to Jody for reading the first chapter of my first book ever and telling me that it didn't suck. This isn't that book, but without that first try, this book wouldn't exist.

And thanks to Kim for being the rock when I can't. You make even the small victories important, and for that, I love you.

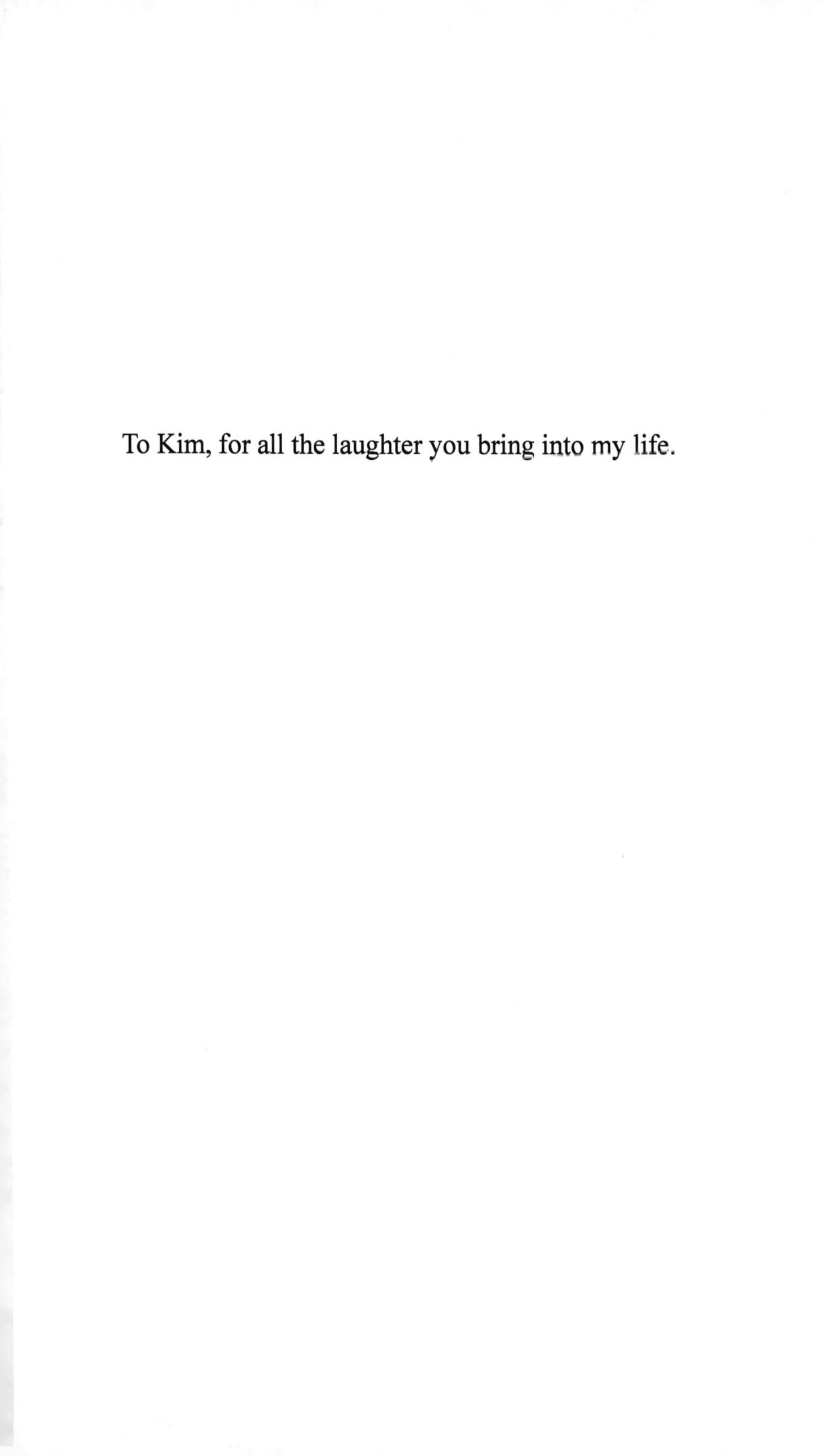

To Kim, for all the laughter you bring into my life.

CHAPTER ONE

Two minutes. A lifetime in a hundred and twenty seconds. It's enough time to save forty-five thousand lives, enough time to end a career. Or both. As first officer of the *Persephone*, my decision to eject an engine core without authorization could be a quick maglev ride to a court martial, but if I succeed, it'll be worth it.

"Did we list?" I yell at Hartley, the head engineer. He doesn't remove his focus from his console, just shakes his head. So, this is Hartley in crisis mode. It's welcoming to see he can play grown-up when needed.

I begin to pull myself up, using the rail surrounding the pit of the engine well, and the ship banks to the left. I lose my balance. My head smashes against the rail, and it takes a moment before my vision clears.

In space, there are any number of anomalies that can throw us for a loop: space debris, asteroids, cosmic dust, gravity wells. The hazards are endless, and the trick is to be prepared.

Hartley shakes his head in exasperation. "Why do you always have to be such a hero, Ash?"

But I'm not a hero.

A small puck-like device—one of Hartley's inventions—careens toward the edge of the well. If it falls over, any hope of ejecting that core will be gone. Without thinking, I reach for it, and when my fingers grip the smooth surface, I realize what a colossal mistake I've made.

I'm the result of happenstance. When I was ten, I remember having to study the Great Migration—when humans fled Earth to the asteroid belt between Mars and Jupiter. A whole series of downloads focused on the role of Angus Shreves, the first captain to land on Ceres (later known as Alpha Station). The way they spoke about him, brave, steadfast and without flaws, made it sound as if he was superhuman. He wasn't. I'd always known him as a hard-of-hearing old man, my quiet and moody grandpa.

A few months before I was set to join the academy, my grandpa once asked me the year the Great Migration started. We were in a cafe on Alpha, just a few years before he died. I knew the answer but doubted myself and named a different year. He nodded in his quiet, gruff way and didn't say anything. I missed my opportunity. Maybe saying the right year would've been a key to learning more about the way he helped change humanity's future. But he never did correct me. Ever.

In truth, I think he kept quiet because it was second nature. For him, it wasn't special to be self-effacing. He wasn't the superhero everyone made him out to be.

Here we go. Sirens have begun to blare all around the engine room.

In seconds, one hundred amps barrel through my fingertips and cut through my system like razor blades. Everything goes hazy. The sirens fade into the background, and chaos erupts in a muted play of colors and sensations.

Hartley grasps at me before I go over. He seizes my arm, and a surge jolts me backward. The only other time I can remember feeling such intensity is with Captain Jordan Kellow. I remember why I'm doing this. Even if I never again get to touch her creamy skin or run my hands through that wild black hair, this last act is for her.

❖

Four weeks earlier

I step over the threshold of the *Persephone* and feel an excitement well up so quick and so fierce, it brings tears to my eyes. I blink fast before the corporal beside me sees and thinks I'm an emotional basket case. *This is it!* The last time I will ever watch the sun rise over the asteroid belt. The last time I will ever see Earth from the giant telescopes on Alpha Station. The last time my dad will ever hug me good-bye. It's a heady feeling, this combination of excitement and sadness, and I swallow it deep.

In less than four weeks we'll dock at the *Posterus*, the first generational ship ever constructed, and begin the most important journey humankind has ever undertaken. More important than discovering fire and creating language. Or even more important than abandoning Earth to live confined in biostations among the asteroid belt over one hundred years ago.

"Lieutenant?" The corporal verbally nudges me. "The captain is this way." He points down a long hallway lit by strips of yellow-tinted LEDs. They're supposed to simulate sunlight but do a poor job on ships this old. Even in the biostations we have sunlight—it's remote and weak, but at least it's real. I hoist my duffel and follow the corporal down the corridor. Our footsteps echo on the metal grates.

From what I remember, the *Persephone* is one of the older ships still in commission, but thanks to a lucky mishap with a stray communications buoy, the engine is new and probably one of the fastest in the Union fleet, traveling at 160,000 kph. That's ten thousand kilometers faster than any other ship in the fleet and more than a hundred times the speed of craft humans first used for space travel. The new engine is the only reason the ship was one of two from the Union fleet selected for this mission.

"I'd like to drop my duffel before we get there." I shift the hemp bag holding everything I own farther up on my shoulder. It's not much, a few books that survived the Great Migration, family pictures, and bits and pieces I've collected from scavengers on their return trips from Earth. Junk that doesn't mean much up here in space, but helps me recreate what life must have once been like on Earth.

The corporal stops and turns. The slump in his posture tells me everything I need to know about what he thinks of my statement. "Your cabin is on the other side of the ship. The captain won't like to be kept waiting."

I don't want to report for duty lugging a lumpy bag coated with ten years of asteroid dust, hard-earned from being dragged from ship to station to ship. My eyes narrow.

He huffs toward the ceiling, his bald head reflecting the yellow of the LEDs flanking us. I hate people who wear their attitude like a badge.

"Tell you what." The duffel drops from my shoulder with a loud thump. "I'll leave it here, and you can deliver it to my cabin after you show me to the captain." I stroll away before he can protest.

The captain's cabin is only three decks up, but the corporal is panting before he's even climbed the chute ladder. I spend the rest of the climb imagining all the fun I'm going to have whipping this crew into shape. He leaves me at her door with a flippant salute. Dick. I bite my tongue and then knock before my fist roams somewhere less professional.

When I enter, I take in everything at once, like watching an instaflash of data dump on my screen. First, I see the knickknacks on every surface, then the view of splayed asteroids from the windows behind the bed. It's unmade, all twisted sheets and tangled duvet. I inhale the scent of apricots, and it conquers my senses. My eyes settle on the woman behind the cluttered desk, and to my chagrin, I am immediately enchanted by her raven hair and milky skin. Captain Jordan Kellow. When her gaze shifts first to the unmade bed, then back to me, my cheeks flush. I force myself to keep eye contact and try to forget that I've just seen such an intimate part of her life. I don't know what it is about seeing the unmade bed, but it unnerves me, and my confidence bolts, leaving me feeling like I'm reporting for my first assignment as a low-ranking aviator.

"I apologize for the mess. We've switched to *Posterus* time already. I want the transition once we get there to be as smooth as possible, but right now it's proving to be a bit of a hiccup." She stretches back in her chair, arms high above her head. The beginnings of a yawn reach her mouth before she clamps down and stifles it.

I sit and know I'm going to embarrass myself somehow. My heartbeat picks up and my system floods with adrenaline. As soon as I sit down, I realize I've already made a mistake. She didn't ask me to be seated. I shoot out of the chair so fast that I knock it over.

For Christ's sake, Ash, calm down. This is no way for a first officer to act. She's going to think I'm spastic.

"Have a seat, Lieutenant," she says, and her voice is like warm honey. She pushes aside the mess on her desk and taps the surface twice to pull up my service file. I cringe as my ID picture materializes in the air between us. I've always hated that picture: my face is pinched as if I've just swallowed a ball of wasabi and am trying to hold in the upcoming explosion. It doesn't even look like me. My auburn hair is pulled back so tight that I look bald, and the flash has washed out my already pale skin, making the constellation of freckles stand out. Thankfully, it disappears as she swishes through several pages to bring up my last assignment.

"How did you like working on the science station?" She sweeps her dark hair back away from her face with her long fingers. She's only half in uniform, and her tunic is unbuttoned. She's wearing what could only be described as pajama pants.

Her bare feet are tucked under her chair, lending credence to her unspoken statement earlier. I've disturbed her sleep.

In truth, I want to shrug because I don't remember much of my time on the Europa Science Station. Five months, and I can't remember more than the first month, but a shrug is not the correct response to that question, so I lie. "It was informative. Colonel Lundy is one of the most efficient officers I've ever had the privilege to work under."

She frowns and I suck in my breath. What else have I forgotten? She flips further back in my service record. "It says here that you called him an ass." Shit. *Did I?* A now familiar sense of panic wells inside me as I realize my memory gaps are more extensive than I initially thought.

"It's okay. I've met Lundy. He is an ass." She raps her knuckles on the desk as if to make it fact and not opinion.

I give a lopsided shrug and grin. "Well, he was an efficient ass." I should just stop speaking.

She laughs, it's quick, so quick, and then she's all business again. When I pictured my new commanding officer, this is not the image I had in mind; this woman is too vibrant, too affable. All the captains I've met have been pompous jackholes.

"I was interested in the filter retrofitting you spearheaded. It's one of the projects I'm going to put you in charge of. I was curious, though, how you managed to get such a large undertaking done in so short a time. You had that whole station finished in less than a month."

"Um…I…" Great stalling tactics, Ash. I should just tell her the truth. *I can't remember the project. Not at all.* But I know I can't because if I do, I'll be left behind. Everything I've worked for, every plan I've made, every goal, every dream will disappear just like my memories into some black hole. I can't let that happen. When I look back at the captain, I will my face not to show my panic. Instead, I shrug. "I guess we didn't have a lot of other things going on at the time."

She leans back in her chair and crosses her arms, scrutinizing me. If that was a test, I don't think I passed. "Lieutenant? Alison? Which do you prefer?"

"Please don't call me Alison. Ali if you must, but I prefer my surname." I squeeze my hands between my legs, aware that it is an entirely unassertive posture, but aware too that if I didn't my hands would be shaking.

She nods. "If this is going to work," she points to herself and to me, "if we're going to work well together, I need your honesty. Everyone on this ship works as a team, including you and me. From what I've read, I don't think I have to worry about you slacking or pulling rank." My mind immediately shifts to the corporal and my duffel sitting three decks below. But I don't have time for regrets as she continues. "I don't want you to feel singled out, because I've made this speech to every crew member on this ship. What we're doing here is momentous, the first of its kind. And I know you've signed all the relevant disclaimers or you wouldn't be here, but even then, very few people can grasp the magnitude of a generational ship and what it means. You and I will never make it to our final destination, we'll be long dead by then. And this here," she motions around her cabin, encompassing our surroundings and the ship as a whole, "this is our home now, and like it or not, we're going to be stuck together for a very long time. We need to work harder at making this work. If this mission is going to succeed, it's not just a matter of getting the ship to its destination, it's about making this new family work, so that those who succeed us make it there as well."

I'm stunned into silence. It's the very real need to distance myself from the shadow my family casts that had me sign up for this mission in the first place. The idea of a new family, one that won't doubt or smother me, is intoxicating.

"It says in your file that you requested transfer a month after you were assigned to the station. What was it about Europa SS that you didn't like?"

I let out the air I've been holding tightly in my chest and search my mind for one honest impression from the experience. I try to picture my room, standing in the lab looking out at Jupiter peaking around Europa, and it hits me, what felt wrong about the place. "I hated standing still, every day with the same view. It felt…wrong."

One brow lifts. It looks almost conspiratorial, like we're sharing a secret need to keep moving. Always moving forward. "Considering our current mission, I think that's a good answer." She regards me from across her desk as if she's working out a puzzle. She hesitates for only a second, then says, "Would you like a tour of the ship?"

Surprised at the offer, I nod and stand. "Captain Kellow? What name do you prefer? Lundy insisted everyone call him sir, although I think if he'd had his way, everyone would've had to call him master." I doubt she's that type, and I know if I were captain I'd hate to be called ma'am.

She barks a laugh as she rounds her desk. "Captain is fine. If you call me ma'am, I'll strap you to the matter sails."

My eyes flick to her bed one last time as we leave. I can't help myself. She sighs and looks pointedly at me. "What is it about the bed that disturbs you, Ash? Please tell me you're not one of those OCD types?"

"I'm just surprised they have your office and private quarters combined as one." It's a half truth. I am surprised, I've never been inside a captain's cabin before, but it's not the reason I find it hard to keep my eyes away from her bed. I keep picturing her lying in it, her black hair splashed across the pillow, wrapped in sleep. It's a consuming thought.

She shrugs as she swipes her hand over her door, locking it. "This is a small ship, and we don't have a lot of room for frivolities." She leads the way down the corridor. "We'll start at the bottom and work our way up."

On the lower deck, she takes me down a long corridor. It's

darker than the others. At the end is a single door. She stops at a panel. "This is kind of cool, actually," she says and taps in a passcode. When the door opens, we're standing in a small antechamber, and in the middle is a ladder leading down. She grabs the top rung and descends. I follow a second later, and when I get to the bottom, my breath catches in my throat. Running the circumference of the ship is a track surrounded by windows that look out into space. Right now, we're still docked at Alpha Station, so there's not much to see, but I can imagine the effect once we're in space.

It will be like running among the stars.

"Cool, huh?" she says as we walk out on the track. I bend down and run my hands along the surface. It feels just like the Tartan Track at Basic Training, rough and soft all at the same time, and when I push down it yields to my touch.

I can't decide if I'm about to laugh or cry as I stand. All I know is that I'll be spending a lot of time here. "I thought the *Persephone* didn't do frivolities."

She scowls in mock seriousness. "Exercise is not a frivolity, Ash, it's a necessity." I wish she'd tell her lower ranks that.

I stroll to the edge to stare out the window at the city buried below the hard thick dome. Lights glow, exaggerated through the shield. This is the last time I will ever see it. I'm barely paying attention, too absorbed in the excitement of leaving.

"Do you have family you're leaving behind?" She dips her head toward the belt splashed before us. I don't say anything, just nod. "Can I ask why you signed up for this mission?"

It's a good question, and I want to answer her honestly because I know she won't take the answer I gave the Union leaders. Or even the answer I gave my father. I can still see the hurt in his eyes when I told him I was applying for the mission. A twinge of guilt invades my happy mood for just a second as I realize that he's the last one. With me gone, he has no one left.

Staying here just feels like failure. Even though I'll never live to see it, I want my grandkids to. I need to believe that one day they will be able to turn their heads toward the sun and soak in its warmth, not through ten feet of metallic glass, but with nothing more between them than the atmosphere and a layer of ozone.

I would be lying, though, if I said this was my only reason. My real reason is much more selfish.

For once in my life, I want to have something that's mine. Just mine. The farther we get from the Milky Way, the less my family's name means anything. Each year we travel, each kilometer, light-year, every sector of unchartered territory gives me back my life. Never again will I have to sit across from my father, his imposing desk between us, and hear how a particular choice or decision of mine will affect his name, our family's name, some stupid legacy that shouldn't even matter. Even though I changed my name before entering the academy, very few people don't know whose daughter I am. It's like being stuck under a rock, the weight of it slowly crushing me.

Out here I'm free. Now that I can feel freedom humming through my body, it's like a drug I never want to kick. I want the high to last the rest of my life. And the irony is, all I had to do to get it was leave everyone I love behind.

Captain Kellow watches a supply train weaving through the stockyards. Somehow I don't think she'd understand.

Instead, I give her a small portion of the truth. "I need to know the human species will move forward. If I stay here, I'll never know."

"You have faith we'll make it to Kepler 980f?"

I cringe at the assigned name of our destination, a planet so far away it might not be the paradise we've made it out to be.

Below us in another dock, a small frigate pulls away, preparing to launch. "I have faith our descendants will." The frigate unfurls its front sails for matter collection. Probably on its way to Europa. Since the attack, most ships are headed there to help with repairs.

"A lot can happen in a hundred years."

"And won't it be exciting?" I twist my fingers together, cracking my knuckles. Tiny sparks of excitement ignite within me, and I feel like I'm five, waiting for Christmas morning to arrive. As much as I'll miss certain aspects—my father, the familiar constellations and planets—I know I won't miss them enough to stay behind. I'd rather spend the rest of my life on a generational ship speeding into the unknown.

Chapter Two

I stand in front of the mirror in my cabin, assessing my formal wear. There's a welcome reception tonight for Hartley and me, and I hate receptions. I suck at small talk and always feel awkward eating off tiny plates. Still, I've made an effort, ditching the traditional dress uniform for a simple backless green dress, cut just above the knees. It shows a hint of cleavage, but not enough to be inappropriate. My hair hangs loose, tickling my back and shoulders. I fasten my necklace, a single black pearl—well, fake pearl—strung by a barely-there chain. It's the only piece of jewelry I own, given to me by my father when I graduated from the academy. He was so proud I'd joined the Union fleet. Personally, I think he was more excited about the leverage he could use in the Commons with a daughter in the service. Maybe that's unfair, but he's always saying you have to find your edge, especially if it's personal. I'll never have to endure one of his for-your-own-good lectures again, and I'm not sure if that saddens me.

I've timed it so I arrive twenty minutes late; the less chitchat I have to endure before they call us to dinner, the better. I stand outside the officers' mess and press the panel on my right, and the door slips open. I spot Hartley first, in the corner by the window surrounded by a bunch of engineer geeks. Since he's the only person I've met besides the captain, I head his way, and he waves as soon as he sees me. The mess is crowded with officers, and with a few crew members bellowing, the excitement is palpable.

Hartley takes my hand and lifts it away from my body to get a better look at my dress. "You look fantastic in that. I was worried you might show up in dress uniform." He pairs his somewhat inappropriate compliment with a face-stretching grin and stuffs a cheese ball in his mouth. If he were Union fleet, it would be wholly inappropriate to speak to a superior officer like that. But Hartley is part of the civilian group included in the mission to fill any knowledge gaps. Only the two Union ships and the *Posterus* crew are Union, the rest are civilians. But Hartley's the only one assigned to our ship.

Ben Hartley has no filter between his brain and mouth. It's the first thing I noticed when I met him at the air dock. He arrived earlier this afternoon with two giant containers, one of which contains the engine core for the *Posterus*, the other with who knows what.

"Would you like to see the engine room or your cabin first?" I asked, shaking his hand.

He grinned wide. "How 'bout your cabin?" He's tall and lanky, pure geek, his confidence doesn't match his looks. I could have made as if I was offended, but I've always hated the sort who can't take a joke or poorly placed compliment.

"It's not that big. I don't think there'd be room for your ego."

His laugh, also incongruous, boomed out of his skinny chest, quick and thunderous. "I think we're going to get along just fine, Lieutenant."

He hands me a champagne flute and stands on his toes, peering over my head. "The heels are a little high, though."

It's entertaining to see that he's still just as cheeky at the reception as he was when I first met him.

"You might want to tone those down," he continues and nods to the men surrounding him, none of whom are as tall or brazen. Only one looks shocked, and the rest are in awe, hanging off his every word as if he were a god.

I've read his file and a few of his papers, so I know that his confidence and this godlike reverence comes from his being the leading mind in nuclear fusion propulsion. He's the reason it will only take one hundred years to get to Kepler 980f instead of five hundred. He's not the only one working on it, but he's the one who solved the containment issue, and all the other problems seemed to fall into place after that.

Uncouth as he is, I decide I like him.

And to prove my point, he slaps my back and points to the others. "Holy crap, where are my manners? Guys, this is Lieutenant Ali Ash, our new first officer. Ash, these are the guys on my team. Well, I guess they're my team now that I'm here. But you know what I mean, these are the engineers on board." He's bouncing on the balls of his feet by this time, barreling through each word so fast I find it hard to keep up. "They're going to help me install the fusion core when we get to the *Posterus*."

I shake each man's hand in turn, trying to remember their names, about to ask if there are any women on the team when Hartley raises his glass to make a toast. I look down at the champagne that I realize I shouldn't have and look for a place to set it without appearing rude. Everyone drinks but me.

Hartley makes a sipping motion with his empty glass. "Aren't you going to join us, Lieutenant?"

"She can't," says a voice close to my ear, and I turn to see Captain Kellow standing beside me. "She's watch staff, which means no alcohol."

Like me, she's opted for civilian formal, and even though her dark blue dress leaves everything to the imagination, it's still gorgeous. Everything about her is a series of contrasts. Sable hair against pale shoulders. Indigo eyes and red lips against her cream-colored complexion.

"I didn't even think about it when it was handed to me, Captain," I stammer. Jesus, I sound like a defensive third-grader.

She takes it from me and hands it to Fukui, one of the engine geeks next to Hartley. "You look like you're behind, Fukui."

Next to the lanky engineer, Fukui looks like one of those anime dolls I've seen among scavengers. All his features appear too tiny for his head, as if they've been squished into the center of his round face.

Kellow has that hint of a smile on her lips, and I can't tell if she's amused by my embarrassment or the situation in general.

Hartley slaps Fukui on the back and yells, "Drink up!"

A canapé drops from his small plate, and I bend to pick it up—I don't know why—and when I stand, Hartley is staring at my cleavage. It takes him a few moments before his eyes rise to mine.

"It's beautiful. Where did you get it?" the captain asks, lightly touching the sphere at my throat.

Instinctively, I reach for my pearl, rolling the silky ball between my fingers. "It was a gift from my father—it's not real," I add. I don't want people to think my family is richer than we are. The only real pearls come from Earth, and the only people who can get to those have credits to burn. Pearl hunting, like everything else on Earth, takes time. If you can find anyone brave enough to descend into the atmosphere, they will spend days maybe even weeks searching the dried waterbeds of the oceans. Personally, I'd rather have my fake.

The dinner chime rings, and like one massive herd everyone pushes toward the other room where they've set up two long tables for dinner. The captain takes my elbow and holds me back. "Can I have a word with you, Lieutenant?" I nod.

She leans in close, and there's something new mixed in with her already familiar scent of apricots, but I can't place it. "Find me after dinner. I'd like to get your first impressions of Hartley," she says.

All I can do is nod.

At dinner, talk turns to the Burrs, as it usually does with this many drinks in everyone. Burrs are our version of space pirates. They're bio-technically enhanced, throwbacks from the resource wars before we left Earth over a hundred years ago.

Most of us living have never even seen Earth, but the majority of Burrs grew up there. They were recruited into armies for various countries—ones which no longer exist—and enhanced. Humans spent their last days on Earth fighting each other, and who better to do that for them than bio-enhanced soldiers, sold to the highest bidder. Just exactly how the soldiers were enhanced was a closely guarded secret by Ethan Burr, the man who pioneered the technology. All that mattered was that they were fast, and strong, and could fight harder and longer than the enemy. In the end, it came down to money. But doesn't it always? The winners were the countries that could afford the best troops, the best tech.

One of the drawbacks of those enhancements, as it turned out, was an extended life span. Burrs living now are over one hundred and twenty years old, but merely look middle-aged. I suspect part of people's resentment comes from that. But a lot of people also hate them because they aren't pure human, not really. When more than half your body is created on an assembly line and not by nature, what does that make you?

After the wars, when they went rogue and began attacking cargo ships and settlements on the belt, the name Burrs, pulled from their creator, just sort of stuck.

"Lieutenant Ash, is it true you were posted on the Europa Science Station when it was attacked?"

I nod. "Yes, I was stationed there for five months." The person who's asked, a sergeant who works with hydroponics, smiles as if I've admitted I shit pearls. I fork another bite of quinoa into my mouth and hope he doesn't ask anything else. But of course, he does.

"Gosh, what was it like being so close to a Burr? Were you scared?"

These are the questions that infuriate me. What do they expect my answer to be? No, I'm used to having terrorists shove guns in my face, I'm used to surviving explosions, used to waking up feeling violated and have no idea why. I mean, of course I was scared, anyone would be. But I'm trained to handle it, and since I'm still alive, I know I worked through the fear. Also, I hate people who use the word *gosh*, only five-year-olds with speech impediments should use it.

I finish chewing, preparing my lie. Everyone around the table has stopped talking amongst themselves and is staring at me. Better make it a good one. "I was in the science lab when the first explosion occurred two decks below. When they did storm our deck, I was already out cold. I got thrown back and was impaled by a soldering arm." I point to my side where I still have a slight scar on my back. The last part is correct; the security cameras were still working until that point. The next part is pure fiction. "What I do remember when I woke up was a lot of smoke and these cold eyes staring at me. And these fingers reaching out to me, but there wasn't any flesh on them, just metal." Everyone is silent as if I've just finished a ghost story. The sergeant shudders. Why can't I just say I don't like talking about it?

"This is horrible. Why hasn't the government done anything about it?" says a woman at the end of the table. The room explodes, everyone talking at once.

"Can't just let them get away with this—"

"A menace."

"Downright creepy the way they just won't die—"

"Thankfully they're sterile."

The noise builds, and each new voice drowns out the last. "Why haven't they been tracked and put down?"

"Because they're human beings." The group turns to Captain

Kellow. Her hands are pressed into the table on either side of her plate as if she's ready to spring out of her chair. "Not rabid dogs."

"Yes, but there has to be checks and balances," says Fukui, his face flushed from drink. "We can't just let them do whatever they want. They've attacked vessels, too. Anyone who tries to go near Earth is a target."

"I agree that something needs to be done." Kellow pauses and studies the group in front of her. I can tell she's mentally editing her next statement. "But what do we become, if not worse monsters? When our preference is extermination? We may not have been the ones to make the decisions that set them on this destructive path, but we're here now, and how we deal with it dictates the kind of society we become." She takes a sip of water, and her slight tremor shows she's restrained half of what she wants to say.

To my right, I hear a sharp barking laugh and turn to see Hartley, a big grin on his face. "Why does it matter? This isn't our problem anymore. In another couple of weeks, we'll have a whole other set of issues to deal with, and lucky for us, that no longer includes the Burrs."

There are nods of agreement, and from the corner of my eye, I see the captain has more to say, but instead she flaps her napkin on the table, bringing the discussion to a close.

CHAPTER THREE

After dinner, I find the captain in her cabin. She's discarded her dress for sweats and piled her hair haphazardly on her head. In this light, it shines almost blue. She beckons me in without a word and takes a seat behind her desk. The surface is spotless. None of the previous stacks of items mar the dark glass. It takes every ounce of my self-control, but I manage not to look over at her bed, which I can see through my peripheral vision has been made.

"What is it about ignorance that breeds fear? Or is it the other way around?" she says, rubbing her forehead.

I can't judge her mood. She's either very tired or, more likely, exasperated. My father used to make a similar gesture right before he was going to chew me out about some indiscretion.

I grip my chair. My entire body has gone rigid.

"When you were assigned here, I was looking forward to working with you." My heart drops into my stomach. This will not end well. "All your former commanders had really great things to say about you." She's silent for so long after, I wonder if it's an intimidation tactic. It should be. It's working.

"But?" I prompt.

She regards me from behind her desk, arms crossed over her sweater obscuring the words "Delta Academy." Her lips are tight. "But after your performance at the reception, I'm not sure what to think."

I smooth the creases along my thighs and cross my legs, buying time, building courage. "Performance?" I hate how quiet my voice is.

"I'm not sure where you pulled that description of a Burr from, but I know it wasn't your memory."

I fidget with the hem of my dress, twisting it between my fingers. The image of a man dressed in black Kevlar jumps from my memory. It's an old memory, much older than the attack on Europa station. But even now, I can still see him clearly. From my angle, he looked almost human. It could've been my uncle, or my neighbor dressed up for a lark. It's when he gets closer that things begin to shift into unreality. His face is far too smooth and doesn't match the matted gray hair hanging lank from his scalp. His eyes are a crisp green but sit too far back in his face, almost as if someone shoved them into a form of clay, but pressed too hard. The terror of it is how closely they resemble us, but how do you put that into words when explaining to someone what it's like to meet a Burr?

I couldn't use that description at dinner, and so I lied. I don't want to build another lie, but I know as soon as anyone finds out about my memory gaps, I'll be sent back to medical and another officer will take my place. I want to trust her, but I'm not that brave. "The truth is, I only remember bits and pieces about the attack."

"Then why don't you just say that?"

Because I'm a bit of a shit. No, that's not entirely accurate. When I first got out of the hospital, I tried to tell people that I couldn't remember anything about the attack, but this only led to more testing. If I hadn't pretended to recover my memories, I'd still be there.

"I apologize, Captain. Next time I won't hesitate to say those words." I've only been here for a day, and I'm already messing up. I know I'm better than this.

Kellow stands and circles her desk and reaches past to grab something from the shelf behind me. She pulls out a glass bottle with amber liquid inside and two tumblers.

"You've been on board for less than a day and already have half the crew intimidated by you. I've had at least six complaints about the new exercise regimen you've enacted."

A small surge of pride wells up in me.

"And you have Hartley eating up whatever you're dishing out. I like the changes and additions you've made to the crew schedule. All these things tell me we're going to work great together, and yet I get this feeling of reserve from you. What is it about me that has you so…standoffish? Is it because I'm a woman? You don't like the idea of taking orders from me?"

"I have no problems taking orders from women." She thinks I'm standoffish? Intimidated, yes, but standoffish?

"So it's me specifically." She nods and pours the amber liquid into glasses and hands me one. I take a whiff, and my sinuses clear at once. Whatever it is, it's potent. I'm not much of a drinker even when I'm not on watch staff. I've discovered the flimsy filter between my brain and mouth dissolves with alcohol.

"Is this a test?" I get her exasperated look again.

"No, Ash. It's not a test. The nature of this mission means our crew is going to have to become a family." She shoves several tablets aside, making room for her to perch on her desk across from me. Her legs are too short to reach the ground, and they swing as she sips her drink. "I'm just trying to get you to open up, maybe relax a little."

I throw the liquid back, and it scorches my throat, making me take a huge gulp of air. *Holy fuck!* "What is this stuff?" The burn spreads to my fingers and toes, leaving a warm glow in its wake.

It takes a minute for her laugh to die. "It's called tequila, and it's from Earth. The plant it's made from doesn't grow too well up here." She holds the bottle out. "Would you like some more?"

No. "Sure." I hold my glass out, and she pours another ounce.

"I think it's meant to be sipped." Her mouth curls around the glass, plumping her bottom lip.

"I want you to know you can say anything you want, Ash. I prefer bluntness. In fact, it's one of the reasons I requested you for this assignment."

"Requested me?"

"I had a list of candidates to choose from, and when I spoke with Colonel Shreves, he said you tended to speak your mind. I like that in a first officer."

I nearly drop my drink, and several emotions race through me at once. The first across the finish line is doubt, followed by gratitude, and the heaviest, coming in last, is anger.

"I don't think he was saying that to recommend me."

"Oh? And why is that?"

I reach for my pearl, grip it in my fist. I want to rip it from my neck and throw it on the ground. "Because Colonel Shreves is my father." The night I told him I wanted to apply for the *Posterus* mission we had one of those excruciating rip-your-heart-out fights, the kind that leaves you emotionally spent for the next couple of days. "He wasn't keen on my coming along for the mission." I take a big gulp of tequila. "And in his vocabulary, 'speak your mind' is synonymous with 'rude.'" I finish the last of my drink and cradle the glass in my lap. Before finishing school, I changed my surname to my mother's because I didn't want my dad's name opening any doors for me, and without even meaning to, he opened the most important one.

She must see at least some of this on my face because she touches my arm lightly. "Hey, you didn't get this assignment because of him. You got it because you worked hard for it."

I blow out a long breath, square my shoulders, and look up

at her. I don't need any handholding. "It doesn't matter how I got the assignment. All that matters is that I'm good at it." The alcohol has moved from my fingertips and lodged in my brain. The outlines of objects in the room are starker, and the colors brighter, even the smell of apricots has intensified. I want to close my eyes and drift away.

"Speaking of which, what are your thoughts on Hartley?" She finishes her drink and corks the bottle before placing it back on the shelf behind me. *From Earth.* It must have cost a fortune.

As I think of the best way to put what I got from meeting Hartley into words, I notice that all the knickknacks are gone, and only a couple of items remain on the shelves. "Well, I get the impression he's spent most of his life wishing he was the big man on campus, and now that he is, it's going to his head a little."

"You think that'll be a problem? We've got a lot of work to do before we arrive at the *Posterus*, and I don't need some prima donna thinking it's beneath him to help install new solar panels and matter collectors." She returns to her perch on the front of her desk. I wonder where she's hidden all her stuff. There isn't a lot of storage space in these cabins, although she's the captain, so maybe she has more storage than others.

"All you have to do is treat him like the stud he thinks he is, and you've got him in your pocket," I say and smile because I can't imagine the captain stroking Hartley's ego.

"Hmm, I'll let you deal with him, if that's all right."

"What did you do with all your stuff?" I'm up and out of my seat before I even realize it. I stop at a shelf running beneath her windows and pick up a small glass orb painted to look like Earth. "You used to have a whole collection of rocks and shells."

She takes the globe from my hand and holds it up to the light. It's painted as Earth used to look, before the oceans receded and the dust storms took over. "I packed them away."

"Why? They were beautiful."

"I was reminded recently that first impressions are important.

With the nature of our mission, I'm going to have to use this as an office more than I was used to." She shrugs and her sweater slips off her shoulder, and I catch a glimpse of her collarbone. Her skin is so smooth and rich, like a pail of milk. If I were to reach out and touch it, I wonder if it would cause ripples. "Besides, this way I have fewer things to dust." She places the globe back on its holder.

"I should probably go. I have first shift tomorrow." I turn to leave, but she touches my arm, holding me back. Her fingertips are icy. The contrast with my warm skin sends a shiver through me.

"About this Hartley thing, Ash, this goes without saying, but no fraternizing with the crew."

I almost choke at the idea of fraternizing with Hartley. I may speak his language, but that doesn't mean I want to. "No, I get that. Don't shit where you eat."

She laughs out loud. It starts deep inside, then resonates around her cabin, sparking every nerve in my body. It's so freeing the way she uses her whole body like she's putting everything she's worth into it, making it count. The sound is deep and throaty, and when it bounces back from around the room, it shudders through me, making me wish I didn't have to leave.

"I like the way you laugh," I say, then immediately wish I could swallow my words. The burn in my cheeks creeps down my neck.

Her dark blue eyes skim every part of my face. Then she grins. It crinkles her eyes, pushing her cheekbones up. I can't tell if it's from pity or amusement.

"Maybe not so much tequila next time," she says.

"Yes, Captain." I nod. The doors whoosh shut behind me, making my ears ring from the silence in the corridor.

Chapter Four

I lose myself in routine. Part of the reason I was chosen for this assignment is my knowledge of energy conservation technologies. Our ship may be fast, but most of the *Persephone*'s technology for matter collection and filtering is a couple of decades out of date. It's my job to create and supervise the teams that will make the necessary changes and updates. Not all of them have to be done in the three weeks it'll take us to get to the *Posterus*, but the installation of our new docking clamp—the longest and hardest task—will need to be complete when we arrive. I've set up three teams, each working eight-hour shifts for every project—ensuring that there are several hopeful epitaphs, involving me, painted in phosphorescent paint around the ship. Hartley is basically my only friend. If he didn't have worshipping geeklings to do all the work I've assigned him, that would change.

I don't sleep much. It's a combination of stress and trying to keep a twenty-four-hour workday. I catch sleep at odd times, but most nights I lie awake staring at my ceiling. By two or three, I'm usually on the track, trying to run myself into exhaustion.

I enter the mess, not surprised to see Hartley sitting by himself, and grab a tray and shovel a heap of soybeans and lentils on my plate, avoiding the miscellaneous pasta and opting for chocolate pudding instead.

"Hartley, how is it that you are the fastest talker I've ever met, but the slowest eater?" I ask, taking a seat across from him.

"Speed is relative," he says and spears a gelatinous globule, meant to represent a meatball, with his fork and shoves it toward his face. It's too large for his mouth. Slime slides off the sides and pools at the corners, which drips down his chin like a Fu Manchu mustache onto his sloppy plate.

"It must take you at least three hours to finish a meal. How do you ever get any work done?"

"But this way I get to eat with everyone." He grins one of his full-face grins, dropping more food on his plate. It splatters on his coveralls. He wipes at it absently, smearing more sauce from his fingers down the front in four long streaks. I don't know what's more disturbing, that it's almost neon red, or that there are mysterious green bits in it.

I look away. As much as I appreciate Hartley's company, he's not always the greatest dinner companion.

The mess is lined with long tables on one side and smaller round tables at our end. I've noticed that at breakfast and lunch people tend to use the longer tables, rarely bothering to sit in groups. These are usually fast meals. But at dinner, the round tables fill up quickly when crew members are usually off-duty and can linger over their food, or shall we say what passes for food on this ship.

As I turn back, my eye catches the captain as she enters the food line.

A second later Hartley notices, too. "Captain!" He waves her over. "We've saved you a seat."

I concentrate on my food, willing my face to behave and stay its normal color. Over the past week, I've only seen her twice, and there was no actual speaking involved. I'm still mortified by my behavior the other night.

She slides in next to me, her knee briefly grazing mine.

"Captain," I say with a nod.

"Impressive work on the docking clamp. I was surprised at your progress considering you've decided to get everything done before we reach the *Posterus*. You know that's not necessary. You don't need to work the crew that hard."

She takes a sip of some orange beverage I made the mistake of trying the other day. It reminded me of feet. Several people have perked up at her comment.

"You're right, it's not necessary," I reply. "But when we get to the *Posterus*, we'll lose Hartley and all of his team for at least a couple of weeks. I thought it best to use the resources we have now and work people at a reasonable pace, instead of waiting until we got to the *Posterus*, where I'd be forced to work everyone overtime." I shrug as if this is common sense. It is of course only half the reason. The other is that I want to show off, prove that I'm good at my job.

She smiles that smile like she's seen through me.

With a fork full of pasta halfway to his mouth, Hartley says, "Ash, no offense, but you look…ashen." He lowers the fork to his plate. "I hate to be the one to tell you this, but you're not well liked. In fact, some of the crew have created a Down with Ash Club. They asked me to join, to which of course I said yes. But only to spy and report back to you." He says it in a matter-of-fact way, but his eyes dart from me to the captain, uncertain of our reaction.

I laugh out loud. I can't help myself. "I bet they have several. Just make sure you joined the most exclusive. Only the best for you, Hartley." If people hate me because I'm doing my job, let them.

Hartley scratches his ginger scruff, one of his nervous habits. "Okay, just thought I should tell you."

A few of Hartley's geeklings arrive, pushing everyone closer together. I scoot farther down, away from Hartley and nearer to the captain. Her leg is warm against mine, and my stomach does an unexpected flip.

For a distraction, I point to the orange drink in her hand. "What is that supposed to be?"

"Orange-flavored water. Did you try it?"

"Regretfully."

She looks down at my plate, which has barely been touched, with its scattered soybeans and lentils. "Not a fan of the cuisine?"

"Is anybody?"

She points at Hartley and his mouth full of pasta. He's deep in conversation about some obscure physics law that has yet to be proven. "I think Hartley likes it."

"Hartley has been eating that same plate for the past two hours, and he's not even half done. I think if anything, that proves he doesn't have working taste buds."

"This is the smallest ship you've served on, isn't it?"

I nod, and watch as one of the mess staff dumps a canister full of soybeans into a bin. They slide easily, followed by a stream of glop at the bottom. It turns my stomach.

"The first ship I ever worked on was so small we had to eat rations." She points to her plate with its tofu meatloaf. "This is gourmet compared to that. God, I can't even remember the last time I ate real meat." I don't know how we got on this topic, but I suddenly want to know something more personal than the last time she ate meat.

"Why did you apply for this mission, Captain? If you don't mind me asking." She takes a few thoughtful bites of tofu loaf, chewing each slowly. I think maybe it's too personal a question and she won't answer, but finally she does.

"I guess I was looking for a fresh start."

Before I can probe more, Hartley breaks into our conversation. "What do you think, Captain?" he asks, still chewing the same mouthful as before. "Do you think the farther out from our solar system we go, the more lawless we'll become, or will we instinctually revert to form and obey the laws of the Union?"

She places her fork down next to her half-finished meal. "I

know a lot of people think the farther we get from the Union, the less the laws will apply. But the farther out we get, the more important those laws will become."

Lunch has reached its peak by this point. The tables have slowly been filling with the crew, and even though there is a low buzz throughout the room as everyone moves through the food line, people have noticeably quieted to listen to our table.

"But isn't it important to create our own laws, based on the society we're building?" I say. "That's why they set up the *Posterus* in sects, isn't it? To make the governing body work for us." Several other tables have now turned their full attention on us. With only the occasional tinkle of cutlery, the mess has gone silent. "I mean, hasn't history taught us that what might work in the beginning won't work forever?" I've always felt that for such an adaptable species, we sure have a hard time with change. Part of what makes this so exciting for me is that we are breaking through our comfort zone not only in space exploration, but in government as well. Because the *Posterus* will have to be self-sustainable as a society as well as a ship, they've set up an entirely new directorate to govern the forty-five thousand people aboard.

There are sixteen sects, each in charge of a different aspect of life, such as food resources, security, crew well-being, engineering, conservation, and our sect, Union fleet, to name a few. There's no real central government on board, just one representative from each section voted on by that sect. While that in itself might not be revolutionary, they've weighted decisions based on knowledge. So if, say, there's a vote on food resources, that sect will get two votes instead of one. Only time and patience will tell us if it works.

"I give it a couple years before the whole thing collapses into chaos."

This from a young master corporal at the next table. I recognize him from the bridge. Alexi Vasa. He's in charge of comms. What is it about communications? I swear every comms officer I've ever served with was named Alexi.

"What is it with you and your anarchy, Vasa?" The captain turns around in her seat. There's a slight upturn at the corner of her mouth.

"I'm only saying humans have a bad track record with communal governments. Greed and materialism win out every time." He shrugs as if to apologize for human nature. "Eventually one sect is going to want more and find a way to get it."

"Give it a chance before you tear it down. Our resilience might surprise you," I say.

He points his fork at me. "You know what happens to optimists, don't you?" He mashes the fork into a pile of tofu loaf, spreading it flat around his plate. "They're the first crushed under the boots of realists."

The captain snorts next to me. "I think you mean *cynics*. No one would ever mistake you for a realist, Vasa." She stands, picking up her tray.

"Well, Vasa, if it's more you want, I'll be the first to offer you the rest of my lunch." I push my tray toward him.

Hartley, the captain, and some others laugh.

The captain rests her other hand on my shoulder and whispers, "Don't waste away on me, Lieutenant," before leaving. I feel the pressure from her hand, a reminder of her presence long after she's gone.

Chapter Five

I reach out and turn off the water in the communal showers above the running track. The silence that follows is eerie. At this hour, I have the place to myself, just another reminder of my isolation. I squeeze the water out of my hair and towel off as I enter the change room. It's not a very large room, but then, we aren't a very large crew. I've never seen anyone else in here. Most of the crew is asleep at three in the morning.

It's better this way. It gives me a chance to unwind without having to watch my back. It's been a week since Hartley told me of my un-fan club. What I initially assumed was a harmless lark to make me aware of their dislike has proved something more. The crew has shown more dedication in their task to unnerve me than in their actual assignments.

I pull on my spare track pants and throw on a shirt before heading up to my cabin. I could shower there, but the communal showers are nicer, and this way I don't have to stalk through the ship, dripping sweat everywhere.

Six decks up and I don't encounter a single person. Sometimes I envy the night crew. There's something peaceful about the silence. When I was first on night watch, during my first assignment on a frigate assigned to patrol inside the belt, I used to climb into one of the forward compartments tucked into the bow and just listen to the hum of the ship. I don't know what it is, but there's something comforting about cruising through space wrapped in the certainty that you're sometimes only inches from the utter stillness of space.

With a swish of my hand I open my cabin doors and stop, my mouth agape, mute in my rage. The place has been trashed. My bed sheets sliced down the middle, parted to reveal the mutilated mattress below, like an autopsy only halfway done. What little I've unpacked has been thrown about the room and my duffel contents dumped on the floor.

I pick up a torn book from my desk. It was one of the last things my mother gave me, an old collection of poems by S.T. Coleridge. On the front, written in ink, is a date: 16 May 45, and a place: Haverford West, Pem, Wales. It was never about the poems, but the connection to a time and place on Earth. This book was printed and purchased in a city in Wales, a name my imagination has turned into a paradise with lush trees dipping their leaves into rushing rivers. The only thing better than seeing an ocean spread before me would be to feel the power of water rushing through my fingers as it swept past.

I place the broken book back on my desk and survey the rest of my room. There are very few things in life I value. Most of the trinkets I've collected over the years were burned when the Europa station was attacked, but the few I do have, I treasure.

I spend the next day in a funk. Keeping to myself. I don't visit the mess or the track. Instead, I hole up on the bridge, hunched over one of the consoles, looking through security footage and the entry log to my cabin. As expected, there's no record of anyone but myself entering since I arrived on board. I know immediately the record has been altered because there is one entrance that should be there and isn't. The corporal who dropped off my duffel on my first day.

That evening, I'm still piecing together my cabin. It's mostly a losing battle, since my mattress still looks like it had a threesome with a Swiss Army knife and a machete. I have a sickening feeling it will take several days to get a new one. I've piled all my ripped uniforms and civilian clothes in the middle of the room. All I have left is the uniform on my back, which was thankfully in the laundry when they slaughtered my closet, and the sweats I was wearing last night. They even tore my underwear drawer to shreds.

There's a knock at the door. Thinking it's Hartley, I don't bother to cover the mess. He'd find out soon enough anyway. But when the doors part, and it's the captain standing on the other side, I wish I had at least shoved the slashed panties and bras in my closet.

Her eyes go wide as her gaze focuses on the mess behind me. "Oh, Ash, what happened?" Her hair is loose, and her uniform jacket is unbuttoned like she's come from off duty. Her appearance matches her tone, soft and feminine.

I have an urge to pull her into the hallway, to stop her from seeing the destruction of my cabin. I don't want her involved. I'll track down the members of the DWA and take great pleasure in throwing each and every one in the brig. And possibly forgetting the entrance code.

"Um, I'm sorry, Captain. I probably should have told you when I signed on board, in my spare time I juggle chain saws. One of them got away from me."

She lifts a gnarled plastic figure, a gift from my cousin, taking in the large crack cutting the word PEZ in half. "Was this the fan club Hartley was talking about at lunch yesterday? He said something about being kicked out."

"Um, I think it's an un-fan club when they don't actually like you. But I can handle this issue, Captain." I take the black-helmeted figure from her and set it back on the desk.

"Ash, this is more than a harmless club. This is destruction." She walks farther into my cabin, spotting the bed. I hear rather than see her reaction, a sharp intake of breath. "This is…"

I take in the sight from her perspective. Seeing it for the first time, it *feels* worse than it looks. I feel like I did when I woke up on Alpha after the attack.

"A violation," she finally says.

I nod. "And I intend to treat this seriously. I'm investigating the incident, and I'll handle it appropriately."

"You shouldn't inquire into this yourself."

"No. But I don't trust anyone but myself to do it."

Slowly, after a few seconds, she nods. I can't risk bringing security in on this, especially after finding the security footage and logs tampered with. This needs to be handled quietly. I also can't let them see how much this is affecting me.

"You know," she says, strolling between the different piles of belongings. One with items I'd like to try to fix, another, the largest, bound for recycling. "You might have more luck with the crew if you got to know them, instead of hiding away, working on projects by yourself."

Two days ago, she'd found me in the cargo bay sorting inventory for the next day's project. A task that should've been assigned to a couple of crew members.

I nod but don't say anything.

We stand there for a few seconds, lost in the utter annihilation of my belongings, when finally, I ask, "Was there something you wanted, Captain?"

She taps the tablet in her hand to her forehead. It's actually kind of adorable. "Oh," she says and passes me the tablet. "This came for you. I should warn you. It's from your father."

"Oh." I'm not sure how to take that. It must have come through an encryption band if she has it. Does that mean I should be worried about what it says? Are they calling me back? Did they figure out that I was lying about what I remembered on Europa SS? "Did you see it?"

"Of course not." Her face softens, and she looks at me like she's trying to tread carefully. "I just...the last time we spoke about your father, you didn't seem…" She sighs and wipes her hand on her pants like she's nervous. "I guess I'm just not sure what kind of relationship you have with your father."

"Oh." I wave her off. "It's fine. It's not like that. He was upset that I wanted to go, but in the end, I made him understand." A laugh bubbles up from within but comes out as a snort instead. "He thinks I'm a bit of a bigmouth who gets myself into trouble because I don't like to back down. Like, ever. He's the same, so…" I bump my fists together. "We butt heads a lot." I set the tablet down next to the figure on my desk. "It's probably a last good-bye or something."

She picks up my torn book of Coleridge poems, running her finger along the jagged edge of a page. "Is this why you weren't at lunch today?" For the past couple of days, we've found ourselves eating lunch at the same time.

I shake my head. "We only have another week or so until we're at the *Posterus.* I want to make sure everything's ready."

"Did you eat dinner?" I'm about to deflect when my stomach betrays me, growling loud enough to be heard on Europa station. "Knowing you, you probably haven't eaten anything all day." The way she says it, playful like, brings a smile to my lips, probably the first all day. It pulls at something buried deep. It's been a long time since someone worried about me. Even if she's only being polite or taking pity on me.

I sigh, knowing I can't lie. "I probably should have, but I just didn't feel like hanging around people today." I shrug, a little embarrassed at the admission. "I promise I'll eat tomorrow."

The captain huffs at this and wraps her slender fingers around my wrist, giving it a light tug. "The last thing I need is for my first officer to waste away on me."

Not until we're out in the hallway do I have the sense to ask where we're going.

"To get you something to eat."

"But all the messes are closed."

"For you, maybe. But being captain has its perks." Her grin is mischievous.

As she watches me inhale my second chocolate pudding cup, her hands tighten around a mug of lemon tea, and she stretches out against the back bench like she owns the place. She doesn't indulge in a late-night snack herself. I wonder if it's because it would be like stealing rations from her crew. From what I've seen, she's very protective of everyone, from the kitchen workers to the officers on her bridge.

"Are you ever sorry? About the promotion to captain?" I ask. I couldn't give a shit about being captain. I've never strived for it, knowing all the mahjong and poker games would be closed to me. They may invite me just to be polite, but I would never be their equal.

The captain looks at me like it's an odd question. "Why would I be sorry about that?"

I guess it's a stupid question. When I first came aboard, I kept expecting her to revert to form. You know the type, those commanding officers who crave power, always striving to further their career. It doesn't matter who they have to shove out of the way. But the more I get to know her, the less she seems like she's captain so she can be in charge. It's more like she feels like she's there to steer us right. Maybe I'm wrong.

I'm almost ashamed to admit why I would never want to be captain. But those dark blue eyes, so earnest, like she honestly can't understand why anyone wouldn't want to do what she does, stare at me over the table, and I want to make her understand. "It's very isolating."

She gazes around the mess. It feels strange, empty like this, without the sounds of regular hours. Then those eyes swing back to me. There's an intensity behind them, and something, somewhere, clenches deep inside me.

CHAPTER SIX

A few days later, I'm in the air dock dressing for a spacewalk with team two. We're beginning the outside installation of the preassembled docking clamp, which will allow our ship, the *Persephone*, to create an airtight seal with the *Posterus.* Our docking assembly works for stationary docking—even stations in orbit—however, the speeds required for the *Posterus* to reach its destination are too great for our current clamping mechanism.

I've populated team two with our best. They'll be coming up behind team one, and I want them to catch any mistakes. As a result, it's usually a very quiet shift. Everyone is focused on their tasks, without much interaction. Most of the team have already exited, just a few stragglers and myself are left, when the captain enters. She stops in the entryway, surveying the room until her eyes land on me. I wonder what she's thinking.

"Hey, Lieutenant," says Cadence Ito, one of the stragglers and one of the only extroverts on the shift. "You need a hand with that?" She points to the nozzle of my air tank, which still needs to be connected to my helmet.

The captain waves her off. "I'll help her with it, Ito, thanks." She strides over to me, her movements precise and stiff, and pulls the airlock shut.

"Thanks, Captain."

I bend down and strap on first my left, then my right boot,

sealing them along the seam of my pants. I've been trying to put myself out there more. After speaking with the captain the other night, I changed my shift so I could work with the crew. Instead of being an absent figure giving orders, I became one of them, working just as hard, if not harder, alongside them. For some crew members, I could man the entire ship and it wouldn't make a difference. But a few have become friendlier toward me.

As soon as Ito exits, the captain's mood shifts, but she's not the playful Jordan Kellow she was the other night. There are frown lines along her brow, and her gaze is on everything but me.

"I heard a rumor that you were working all three shifts. Is that true?" The way she says it, as if I've disappointed her, grabs my heart in a vise. She picks up my air tank to pre-check it for me. She swipes her hand over the digital display. It lights up, showing a full tank of air.

I shrug into the arms of my suit and fasten the clasps up the front. "Only a couple hours on each." I wait as the last of the crew leave the air dock before continuing. "I'm just trying to follow your advice, getting to know them, letting them see me work." I grab my gloves but don't put them on, drawing out time. "It seems to be working."

"Yes. But working every shift is extreme. If you're going to risk your safety climbing around the ship, you're going to have to pick one shift. I don't need you burned out before we even reach the *Posterus*."

My chest feels heavy as if my suit is pressing in, squeezing the air out of my lungs. "Is that an order?" I can't believe this is the same person from the other night. The one who snuck us into the mess after hours. The one who watched me scarf down a bowl of pasta and two helpings of chocolate pudding, telling me stories about her first assignment, trying to lift my mood. For the first time, I got a glimpse of the woman behind the rank.

Now, she's closed herself up like a flower I once saw in a vid-stream, protecting itself. It's as if she's folded in on herself.

I'm seeing the captain, not Jordan. And it's not just that she's about to give me a direct order, it's everything about her. It's the way she stands rigid, as if she's afraid to move and expose any flaw in her shield. It's the way she averts her eyes, refusing to show me what she's really feeling.

She folds her arms. "I don't want to have to give you an order, Ash." She rolls her eyes to the ceiling as she says it. When she finally lowers her gaze to mine, she's not just disappointed, she's upset. She starts to say something but stops herself. "When do you sleep?"

"I'm getting along fine." They only delivered a new mattress last night. Even then, as exhausted as I was, I could only close my eyes for an hour.

This isn't the first time I've gotten this reaction. What people don't seem to understand is that I will do almost anything to get a job done. There isn't a rule that's been written I'm not willing to bend, a crew member or officer I'm afraid to go around or bribe or cajole to get results. I've never seen a straight line between myself and my goals. Usually I take a very twisty, bendy route to get there.

The longer we stand staring at each other, the tighter my chest feels. Adrenaline floods my system. I'm ready to fight this. I'm willing to win if I need to. I've never disobeyed a direct order, but I'm also not used to my commanding officers second-guessing my actions, especially when they get results. We are way ahead of schedule, and while I won't hold out for excitement, at least everyone seems to have calmed down.

She takes my gloves from me. Even with my boots on, she's still taller. "Ash, there are two things I will not tolerate on my ship: One is an officer who can't take orders, and the second is any member of my crew who takes actions that will put them or others in danger." She opens the right glove for me to slide my hand in. "And right now you're close to violating both." She fastens the right glove to my suit and opens the left. I slip my hand in, never taking my eyes off her. "Because of that, I'm ordering you to stop working three shifts and to choose just one."

If she'd slapped me in the face, I couldn't be more stunned.

She fastens my left glove to the suit. I'm about to protest, but she takes my helmet and places it over my head, ending the discussion.

❖

I wake up on the med deck with that same pressure of panic as before. I have no idea how I got here or what happened to me. The last thing I remember is the captain placing a helmet over my head. Everything else is a black hole. Shit.

I try to sit up but get pushed back down by a strong, hairy hand. "Not so fast, Lieutenant."

"How long have I been here?" I'm wearing a medical gown, and there are several sensors stuck to my arms and chest.

"Only a few hours," says Dr. Len Prashad.

I met him during my medical when I first signed on board. He swipes a screen to his right, bringing up my vitals. His broad, stocky shoulders are hunched over slightly, the intensity of his observations evident. The blue glow from the screen paints his deep brown skin an eerie color.

"What happened?" I create a mental checklist of all the things I did on the last two spacewalks, all the protocols I followed, and find nothing that would cause an accident. Whatever happened must be external, but I'm the only patient in here.

"You don't remember?"

I shake my head.

His fingers glide over the screen, endless points of data—heart rate, blood pressure, brain chemicals—flash past. "Your body shut down."

"Shut down? What does that mean? Did I pass out?" *Please tell me I didn't faint*. I try to sit up again, but he places a hand on my shoulder, keeping me flat on the bed. His face is kind, and deep wrinkles branch out from the corners of his eyes. He's one of the exceptions to the age restriction; I'd place him in his early fifties. Everyone else on board is thirty-five and under. I wonder if that makes him feel out of place.

"I can't describe it better than that. Corporal Ito will be here shortly to explain the events. What I can tell you, though," he waves a screen with several bar charts into place and points to one of the lines, "is that your cortisol levels are abnormally high." He must see the confusion on my face and smiles. "It's a chemical your adrenal gland makes in times of stress. I've checked your previous medical records, and this is new. I wouldn't be too worried. Prolonged exposure will suppress your immune system, though, among other things." He waves his hand, and another screen slides into view. "You also have very low serotonin levels and high dopamine levels. Have you been having trouble sleeping?"

I nod. None of this tells me anything I want to know. "What's wrong with me?"

He chuckles. "In a word? Stressed. Your body is reacting the only way it knows how. It's releasing all sorts of chemicals to counteract your anxiety, and as a result, other chemicals are being suppressed, which is what's causing your insomnia." He reaches out and removes a sensor from my right temple. "Most of this can be regulated through diet. I'll make a note in your file which foods will help." He makes quick work of removing the other sensors and helps me sit up. "The other thing is your work schedule."

I groan, "Not you, too." My work schedule is the only thing keeping me sane. When I'm not working, my mind races out of control.

He sits down next to me and his head barely reaches my shoulders. "Let me guess, you're working yourself exhausted because it's the only way you can get to sleep when you need it? And when you're not working you feel like you're not doing enough, so you find more to do to calm it all down. Trust me when I say this, if you slow down and manage your diet better, that feeling will go away. It feels counterproductive, but self-medicating with more work is actually causing the issue in the first place."

I debate whether to tell him what's really causing my anxiety. Maybe he'll be more understanding than the doctors on Alpha. I push that thought out the minute Ito walks in.

"Lieutenant! Thank God you're okay."

"What happened?" I feel like I might punch something or someone if I don't find out soon.

She shakes her head and frowns. "It was strange. Everything was going fine. We were almost done and then…" She pauses, hands folded across her chest, eyes raised to the ceiling searching for words. "You started—you grabbed one of the Allen wrenches and began dismantling one of the locking clamps as if you were trying to take it apart. And before anyone could reach you, you just sort of shut down."

I stare at her, realize my mouth has fallen open, and shut it. I lick my lips. My mouth has gone dry. This doesn't even sound like me. "I passed out?" A million emotions surge through me: fear, confusion, anxiety, and most prominent, embarrassment.

"I guess so. Thankfully, you were tethered to the ship. We had to pull you back in, and you were definitely unconscious." Is it pity or sympathy I see on her face? I'm not sure, but I don't welcome either.

I turn to Dr. Prashad. "Am I free to go?"

He nods but gives me a warning list of dos and don'ts. Also, he tells me I've been pulled from active duty for the next two days.

That night I stare at my ceiling, forcing myself to remember something, anything from those missing forty-five minutes. Why was I trying to dismantle the locking clamp? And more to the point, what happened on Europa SS? It's been two months, and I still can't remember anything more than the first month there.

I can't lie still another moment. The doctor said I couldn't perform duties for the next two days, he didn't say anything about running.

I slip on running shoes, shorts, and a T-shirt. I grab my towel and bag. As I swipe my door locked, I notice the clock on my bedside table. It reads zero three hundred. Good, I'll have the track to myself.

I ease into my run, letting my muscles warm gradually through the first few laps. The stars stand in stark contrast to the surrounding space, like tiny pinpricks in a black sheet. With the lights dimmed on the ship, it is almost like running through space. I feel as if I could reach my hand out and touch the glowing spheres. Like cupping a million tiny worlds.

When I was little, my mom used to sing to me. The one I would request most often was "Twinkle, Twinkle Little Star," an old Earth song her grandmother sang to her when she was little. I used to imagine that I was the little girl sitting at my bedroom window, looking up at the stars, wondering what they were. I wanted to see them twinkle. I'd only ever seen them through three meters of metallic glass. Up here, where there's no atmosphere and turbulence to refract the star's light, they never even scintillate. Maybe one day my grandkids will hear that song, and not have to wonder what a twinkling star looks like.

When I get back to my cabin, I throw my bag and fling myself on my bed, fully clothed. As my head hits the pillow, my eyes close, and I sleep. Real sleep. Like I'm dead.

When I wake, I'm in an unfamiliar white room, and my heart slams against my chest. My mind and body are awake in an instant. I sit up and see that I know exactly where I am. I've seen it once before on the tour the captain gave me. I'm in the brig.

CHAPTER SEVEN

I lie on the bed, feet propped up on the wall, hands resting on my chest. I've been here long enough that I'm missing the soybeans and lentils from the mess. My stomach growls just to rub in how hungry I am. I've already banged on the door until my knuckles bled. I've screamed until my throat collapsed. I've plugged the camera hole above the door with a combination of spit and a ripped section of sheet. But still, no one's come.

Now I lie here with a full mind and no answers. I have no explanation for how I ended up here. The last thing I remember is falling on my bed exhausted.

Several more hours pass, at least, I feel they do. And just when I think I could die of boredom, I hear someone on the other side of the door. I sit up hoping I'll finally get answers. But when it swishes open, it's that dick corporal who first showed me to the captain's quarters. He's carrying a food tray with a large helping of soybeans, lentils, and a beef stew concoction that I know will be made of tofu. The smell meets my empty stomach, which crows in greeting.

He leans against the door frame. The smirk he gives me pulls at a dark purple bruise along his jaw, and he doesn't speak or place the tray on the ground. He just watches me for several minutes. I stare back. He makes a weird guttural noise in the back of his throat, spits in my food, and leaves the tray on the floor.

What the hell is happening? Any theories I had just died with that—I don't even know what to call that. That's not payback for adding an exercise regime to his schedule.

I don't bother with the food. Instead I lie back down, place my feet back on the wall, and wait. It's not long before I hear the door slide open again. I continue to stare at the ceiling. Until I hear her voice.

"Lieutenant."

I whirl into a sitting position. The captain is standing in the hallway, her hand gripping the frame as if she's afraid to enter. She looks exhausted. There are dark smudges under her eyes, made all the more prominent by her pale skin. And her hair, which is usually styled tightly into a French twist, has been pulled back into a lazy ponytail.

"What am I doing here?" I say it so quietly. But I want to shout it, to scream it in her face.

She nods to someone outside the room and steps inside. The door closes behind her.

"What am I doing here?" I say it again, more forcefully this time.

She leans against the door, her hands looped behind her back. "You don't remember?" She looks down at the untouched tray of food and back to me.

I take a deep breath and hug my legs to my chest. I'm in the brig, most of me doesn't want to remember. I shake my head. "The last thing I remember is leaving the change room and heading to my cabin to sleep."

"That's the last thing you remember?" Her eyebrows arch, an incredulous look on her face.

Oh, God. "I woke up here." Does this have something to do with my attempt to dismantle the locking clamp? Did they find out why? My whole body is vibrating like it's going to tear apart from the inside.

She pushes off the wall and sinks onto the bed next to me,

hooking her leg to face me. "You've been here, unconscious, for two days."

I grab her arm, forcing her to look at me. "Why am I in here?"

"You attacked Hartley."

"I what?" I let go. I don't believe her. "Why would I attack Hartley? Is he okay?" Please let him be okay.

She nods. "He's fine. Dr. Prashad cleared him for duty a day ago." There's something more she wants to add, her mouth even opens to say it, but she closes it again.

I spring off the bed and slap the opposite wall of the cell. The vibrations have gotten worse. I'm full of restless energy like my panic is a star building toward supernova. "Shit, shit, shit." I start pacing. I need it out, if not, it's going to explode.

"You have no idea why you attacked him?" She clasps her hands in her lap, watching me like I'm a pendulum on a clock.

I'm still pacing, brushing each wall with my fingers as I pass. Trying to remember. But all I get is a black hole. "He's the only person on this ship who truly likes me. Why would I ruin that by attacking him?"

"That's not true." She looks like she wants to say more, but right now I can't hear it.

And that's when I notice. How did I get in uniform? I look down. Even my boots are latched. My black pants are tucked into them, my blue tunic buttoned up my throat. I run my hands down the front. There's blood on one of my sleeves. Is it Hartley's?

"The last thing you remember is getting to your cabin? You remember everything that happened before then?" The tightness of her voice, her posture, everything in her manner, tells me she doesn't believe a word I'm saying.

"I remember being ordered to stop doing my job." It's childish, I know, but I can't help myself. I'm terrified and frustrated.

She rolls her eyes at me like I'm a teenager arguing over

curfew. “I didn’t ask you to stop doing your job, only the job of half the crew.”

“It’s like I’ve been sleepwalking and ended up here with no idea how.” I rub my knuckles, encrusted blood flakes off.

“I find it hard to believe that you can’t remember anything. You weren’t exactly passive. You put Hartley and two security guards in the med center.”

I nudge the food tray with my boot. “One of those wouldn’t happen to be the guy who just brought me my food, would it?”

“You elbowed him in the jaw.”

“Is that all?” He needs to learn how to take a punch.

“Come on.” She stands and beckons toward the door. “Dr. Prashad wants to take a look at you.” She knocks, and it clicks and swishes open. Two security guards sit at a post on the other side of the door. Both are watching us.

“And if I don’t want to go?”

She grabs my elbow and pushes me through the door. “It’s not a request. We want to figure out what’s going on as much as you do, Ash.”

I unbutton my tunic. Dr. Prashad ordered the security guards to wait outside, so it’s only the doctor, the captain, and Chloe—Dr. Prashad’s nurse. She tucks herself into a corner, gripping an empty instrument tray to her chest, her face as pale as her hair.

I’m still nervous. What are they going to find? I shrug off my jacket and fold it over a chair. I bend and unlatch my boots, slipping them off from the heel and placing each under the chair. “How far do you want me to go?”

“The pants, too. I’ll need access to your hip.” Dr. Prashad is busy arranging tools on a tray next to the bed.

I unbutton my pants and slip them down my legs. I wouldn’t usually call myself self-conscious. You kind of lose that part of yourself during basic training. I guess showering with twenty people and only one showerhead will do that. Both the captain and Chloe are watching me undress like I’m about to sprout two heads. Thank God, I had the foresight to put on a nice pair of underwear. It's nerve-wracking when you don't remember. I fold my pants and place them over my tunic and roll off both my socks and ball them into my boots. I sit on the bed in my undershirt and underwear.

Dr. Prashad lifts a black cube between gloved fingers, so tiny I can hardly see it. "I'm going to insert this in at your hip. It will travel to the base of your spine and then up until it reaches your brain stem. It has a camera here," he points to a spot I can't see with his pinkie, "and these sensors," he holds it in his palm so I can get a better look at the sides, "will relay data back to this console." He places it back on the tray and picks up a large syringe. "I need you to lie down now."

I don't budge. "What is that?"

He shows me the capsule he's placed in the holder like I'm supposed to understand what it means. "It'll put you out for the procedure."

I'm already shaking my head before he's finished. "No. I don't want to be put out. I want to know what's going on." Terror surges from my center to the tips of my fingers. The way I feel right now, I don't ever want to sleep again.

He touches my arm. With me sitting and him standing, we're at eye level. "It's very painful. You don't want to be awake for it." He has kind eyes, and I know I should trust him, but I don't. I can't even trust myself right now. I grip the bed and stare wide-eyed.

Chloe busies herself at the monitor setting up the parameters of my vitals on the console. The captain hasn't moved since we entered. She stands just to the side, leaning against the wall.

"I'd rather have the pain than not know what's going on," I say.

"You'll know what we know as soon as you're awake." He tries to ease me down.

"No." I jump off the bed and back myself into a corner, facing him and the captain. I must look like a kid afraid of needles. Even though I'm in my underwear, I'll fight anyone who tries to come near me. I will not let them put me under. I search around for something to grab and use as a weapon. The only thing I have to work with is a chair. It's hard metal. I might get one down. I'll go for the captain first. She's the only one here who's a threat. I know I can take the doctor and Chloe without any problems.

The captain lifts off the wall. She doesn't approach me, though. Instead she turns to the doctor. "Can you do it without putting her to sleep?" She keeps her eyes on me the whole time. Is she afraid I'm going to attack?

He looks aghast. His mouth drops open like he couldn't imagine such a thing.

Shit, this is going to hurt. "Please?" I'm not above a little begging.

He shakes his head like he's saying no, but puts the syringe back on his tray. "Fine." He's still shaking his head, and I realize it's in exasperation. I tend to have that effect on people.

CHAPTER EIGHT

I lean back on the exam bed but don't close my eyes, even though I want to. When I was a kid, my cousin and I used to play this game. Late at night we would sneak out to the animal compounds on the far edge of the station. Each pen was surrounded by electrical fences to keep the animals from wandering off. The voltage wasn't enough to kill you, but it was sufficient to hurt like a bitch and give you a raging headache. The first to chicken out would have to do the other's chores for a week. I always won. Not because I was braver. I won because I didn't think before I did it. I would just grab the fence and hold on, breathing through the pain.

This will hurt. And I have no control over the procedure. That's what scares me the most.

Dr. Prashad places a supportive hand on my shoulder. "If you insist on being awake, you should probably switch to your stomach. You won't feel the pressure on your back as much."

I know he's just trying to help, but I can't turn over. "I'm okay like this."

"Fine, then." He pulls the edge of my underwear down and swabs my hip. Chloe passes him a scalpel. It pauses a few centimeters from my skin. "You're sure you don't want to change your mind?"

"Just do it already," I say through my teeth. My hands have already gripped the edge of the bed in anticipation.

He huffs out a long breath. "Don't move." And without any more hesitation, he slices into my hip.

The scalpel bites into my skin. It's excruciating. My chest heaves and I clamp my teeth together, grinding against the pain. Chloe swabs the cut and passes Dr. Prashad a jaw-like device, which he slips into the opening on my hip and thrusts open.

Holy fuck! My vision blurs. I let out a sound very much like a whimper.

The captain pries my hand from the edge of the bed and clasps it tight. Her fingers wrap around mine. I squeeze hard. I'm breathing fast and shallow now. There's talking, but I only make out part of what they're saying. Dr. Prashad says something about hyperventilating, and I feel rather than see the captain put her hand on my chest. Everything slows.

"Just focus on me," she says.

A coolness radiates throughout my chest, beginning from her palm. The pressure of it has a soothing, almost hypnotic effect. I turn all my attention to her ocean blue eyes, and there's something behind them, something I never noticed before. It makes me feel as if I am being tethered to a ship. And I want to believe it's a connection that she feels, too. Even if I know it's stupid to hope. But more than that, I know it's stupid to want.

"Okay. I'm inserting the diagnostic cube into your hip, then I will sew you up."

I feel the sting of it slipping in, and then a strange sensation as it travels toward the base of my spine.

The captain's eyes dart to something in the doctor's hand. They widen, and I turn to see. He's holding a large curved suture needle threaded with thick, dark thread.

She pulls my hand to her chest. "Look at me." She steps closer to the table, leans in, and says, "It's almost over. Just this last bit."

I breathe in hoping for her scent, apricots and soap, but Dr. Prashad makes his first stitch and all my senses realign to the stabbing pain in my hip. I scrunch my eyes shut and breathe, sucking in through my nose deep enough that the air hits the back of my throat. I focus on this and only this. One breath. One stitch. The captain lifts her hand from my chest, and I feel the absence like a physical ache.

There's a tug on my side as Dr. Prashad ties off the last stitch.

And then I scream.

I can only focus on the pain rampaging through every millimeter of my body. There's nothing to brace against, grit against, rage against. I'm at its mercy. I don't know how long it lasts, but when it clears, my muscles ache from clenching for so long. Rivers of sweat cascade between my breasts, down my arms, from my armpits. I start to shiver. Convulsions pulse through me.

"What's happening to her?" asks the captain.

"I told you this was painful." He takes a thermal blanket from Chloe's outstretched arms and wraps it tight around my body, tucking the edges. "To get to the brain stem, the cube has to climb up her spine, which shelters the spinal nerves. This is the resulting shock of having every nerve along your spine yanked back like the reins on a horse."

Chloe drops a tray with a loud clang. "Oh, my God." Her hand shoots to her mouth. "She's one of them."

I turn to the monitor to see what's happening. "One of who?" I croak. My throat feels raspy and sore, like I've swallowed a pine cone. I can't make any sense of what I'm seeing. The screen is dark except for a small nodule drifting within a nerve clump, like a small ship floating in a nebula. It's beautiful.

Chloe backs away from the bed toward the door. "She's a Burr. They've come." She shakes her head, almost in tears. "They've come, and they're going to destroy us."

Dr. Prashad turns to the monitor and enlarges part of the

screen, focusing on the nodule. It takes me a moment to put it all together, that we are viewing the inside of my body, and that the nodule on the screen is floating inside me. Even with the thermal blanket cocooned around me, I shudder. Two questions immediately form in my mind: How did it get there? And how the hell do I get it out?

"Calm down, Chloe. She can't be a Burr. She's too young, for one." The captain steers her back toward the dropped tray. "Here, let me help you pick this up."

"Well, Captain. I'm impressed. It looks like you were right," says Dr. Prashad.

"Right about what?" I struggle to get untangled and sit upright on the bed. "What is that thing?"

"This right here," he taps the screen, "is an antique. Quite a beautiful piece of tech, too. They really knew how to design back then." He squints up at the nodule, which is slowly rotating inside me somewhere.

"It's called a mind knot, and it was designed a couple of centuries ago by the military as a way to control soldiers' minds. They had this notion of one army, one goal, one mind. The last time it was used was during the resource wars on Earth." His excitement at seeing the mind knot is immediately dimmed the second he looks over at me. It hits home that the knot is inside me, and he averts his eyes and begins transferring notes to a small tablet in his hand.

The mind knot turns to the left, and I see a glowing red ball, like an eye staring out at me, on one side.

"Would you look at that?" Dr. Prashad's voice takes on a soothing effect like he's slipped into another world, and we're not in it. "They've modified the original design."

I finally break free of the blanket and sit up, but it's too quick. My vision rotates, and I feel like I'm going to throw up. I steady myself for a moment before jumping off the bed. My left hip jolts as my feet hit the floor. I hobble over to the monitor to get a closer look at what has Dr. Prashad so fascinated.

"This thing controls minds? It's controlling my mind?" I find that hard to believe. How can something be controlling me when I can't even feel it? I guess that's the point.

"In a way, yes. Its main design feature was to relay orders to soldiers while they were in a state of unconsciousness."

The captain walks over to the monitor and swipes her hand down the length of the screen. A new image comes up, showing the underside of the mind knot. Four orangey-red cords snake out from underneath, stretching like feelers looking for something to grab. "They're meant to take over when the subject shows any pushback."

How does she know so much about them? She zooms out, following the strands. All four are twisted into my brain stem, like parasites leeching off my memories.

I grope the back of my neck as if I might be able to feel the mind knot working away and be able to claw it out. "How do we remove this thing?"

They both turn and stare at me as if I've just suggested we strip naked and run through the corridors with streamers.

Dr. Prashad heaves a sigh as if he's about to tell me humans never actually lived on Earth, and it's only a bedtime story parents tell their children so they won't be afraid of the dark. "It can't be removed. These fibers you see here," he points to the four long strands clamping around my brain stem, "they're bio-synthetic. And once they connect with your brain stem, they mold to your DNA. If I were to try to remove them, it would be like severing your spinal column from your brain stem. You would die instantly."

As he says the word *instantly*, my whole body chills. There has to be some other way.

"Can't you just turn it off?" I don't want to walk around

with someone else's toy inside me for the rest of my life. But worse would be having it still running. I would rather die than be a puppet. I can't live with the fear of never knowing when they could take over my body or use me as a power tool.

"It doesn't work like that. It's acting as an intermediary between your brain and the rest of your nervous system. It would be like turning off your heart. All blood flow would cease, and you would no longer be able to function."

So, that's a *no*.

"What I don't understand is how they implanted it into your system without it being noticed. There would be a large scar and traces of recent surgery," he says.

I lift up my undershirt and feel around the right side of my back. My fingers gloss over the raised skin of my scar from the attack. I turn and show him. "Would this be large enough?"

He bends to inspect my scar. "This is from Europa Station?" His hand glides over the incision, but he doesn't touch it, as if he's afraid of what the mark represents. There's a mixture of awe and fear in his voice. The scientist in him is fascinated, but the human is anxious about the outcome.

I nod. I've never gotten a good look at it myself, but I know it's at least five centimeters long. "When the first ship arrived, they found me unconscious in the med center. I must have made my way down there and patched myself up." But maybe I didn't. That's all part of the black hole now.

"It's a good possibility that when the Burrs attacked the station, they implanted the mind knot. Your injury would have masked any trace," he says, fidgeting with one of the syringe holders on his tray.

The captain is just as nervous. She hasn't taken her eyes off me the entire time, as if she's afraid I'll go on a rampage.

I sit back down on the bed, suddenly feeling woozy. "Why would the Burrs choose me? What is it about me that would make me controllable?" I want to scream out, but if there's one thing my father drilled into me from the time I could listen, it's that life isn't fair. His philosophy was pretty much *life doesn't give handouts, so you need to take what you want.* And it didn't matter who it hurt.

"I'm guessing it has something to do with Hartley. You did attack him, after all."

"But you said he was okay. I didn't hurt him." Why would the Burrs want Hartley dead? If they're trying to stop the mission, it's not like he's the only engineer on board who understands the *Posterus*'s new engine.

"Doctor, you said the mind knot had been modified. What did you mean by that?" The captain still has her face up to the screen, studying the revolving nodule.

"It has a transmitter. The original only had receivers. This was designed to send messages back."

CHAPTER NINE

There's a wrongness skulking deep inside me, hiding since I was a child listening to my cousin Edward's stories. Stories that no child should know, let alone share. Stories that make you grow up too fast, a wickedness that keeps the dark dreams company.

At the time, I believed Edward. I believed some monsters took advantage of us, leeched off us, slaughtered us in the deepness of our nightmares. I believed in them because they were true. I'd seen them. But they weren't monsters. They were us. They were human. When I cringe at the name Burr, share an awful story, when I speak of them like animals, I am every ignorant crew member on this ship, every closed-minded MP in the Commons. I am my father. I am a bigot.

The panic consumes me, tapping at my walls of denial.

I now have the knowledge to go with my fears. I have been violated. Part of me has been lost forever. I am one of the monsters who haunt our nighttime. One of the butchers who attack our way of life. I am now connected to the people who murdered my mother.

I sit in the middle of my bed, hugging my knees. I've been in this position for the past three hours, and I don't plan on moving for another two. I've been confined to my cabin for the previous two days, waiting as the doctor examines the rest of the data he pulled from the diagnostic cube—which I'm told is currently dissolving and working its way through my digestive system. That's a nice thought.

There's a knock at my door. I don't bother to move. I know it will be the corporal with a tray of food to leave with the growing pile next to my door. I stare between my knees and wait for him to leave.

"Lieutenant." It's her.

My stomach floats to the surface. I don't want it to. I want to stay in my funk.

"What is this?" The captain points to the scattered uneaten trays blocking my door. "A hunger strike?"

I shrug, but otherwise, don't move. I'm moping, feeling sorry for myself, and I hate this attitude in other people, but self-pity is a perpetual motion machine. Once it's started, it will keep going and going without any outside effort.

"You have to eat."

I probably would have, I'm starving. But apparently, I'd rather die than eat that dick's spit.

I hear a scraping sound and look up. She's placed a tray of food on my desk. It's not lentils or soybeans either. There's a heaping pile of pasta and meatloaf. She picks up a canister of liquid and offers it to me. That's when I notice the chocolate pudding. She's brought me dessert. I think I could kiss her just for that.

"I'm reinstating you to active duty, Ash. Although no more spacewalks, and you will pick one shift, not three."

My heart soars. Finally. I need to get out of this room the same way Hartley needs to get laid, desperately and immediately.

"So you're not sending me back?" I open the canister and take a sip and almost retch. It's a close approximation to pear juice. I've never had an aversion to pears before, but for some reason, this turns my stomach. As thirsty as I am, I can't make myself drink. It must have something to do with the artificial flavors they use.

"Why would you think that?" She drops a tablet on the bed next to me.

Her uniform is crisp. I can even see pressed seams down the arms of her tunic. She looks better than when I saw her last. Her hair is back in a French twist, and her face is slightly flushed as if she's been working out. I envy her freedom.

"Because I have a stowaway that at any moment could go supernova," I say and swipe the tablet. It flicks to life. It's a data dump from the doctor. I scroll through. He was thorough. There are over one hundred pages of data, all about the intruder lurking in my brain stem.

She pulls my chair out and pushes the tray of food closer. I get the point: Eat while we're talking.

"Dr. Prashad isn't worried and so neither am I. Based on what's happened so far, your body has a pushback mechanism. Both times you've shut down before anything serious happened. Besides, it has a limited range. They've probably hacked into communications buoys to get the signal this far. But once we set out on the *Posterus*, they won't be able to connect to it."

Maybe it's paranoia, but I'm not convinced. They didn't go to all this trouble to be defeated by distance.

I take a seat and unwrap my utensils. It even smells good today.

She circles my cabin, fondling objects. I don't own much, especially after that last trip to recycling. She stops at my duffel and fishes out a picture of Edward and me. It was taken right before I shipped off to basic training. "Who is this?"

"My cousin, Edward."

"You have a cousin?" Not many people do. But then, not many people have siblings on account of the one-child law. He's like a brother, only a year older than me. When we were growing up, everything was a competition: who got better grades in school, who was better in sports. We even had an unofficial contest to see who would lose their virginity first. He claimed Trisha Blake took his on his seventeenth birthday on his living room couch when his mom was at work. But this was never confirmed by Trisha, who I had fifth-period science with. It's possible she was lying to protect her nonexistent reputation. I didn't have the heart to tell him I'd lost it a year earlier, also with Trisha. But that was the thing about Edward. It never mattered if you won, he'd find a way to beat you in the end, by either one-upping you or coming up with something else to compete for.

"My mom was a twin." It's one of two ways around the law. The other is to buy an unwanted. Each family gets a birth card. If for some reason the family decides they don't want to bear children, they may sell their birth card. When you sell your card, they sterilize you.

"Oh, I'm sorry."

"What for?" I hoist a fork full of pasta into my mouth. I know it's only my imagination, but this tastes like the best whatever kind of pasta this is I've ever had.

She places the picture back in my duffel. It's the only picture I have left of him. "You said 'was.' I just assumed…"

There aren't any pictures of my mom and me. I have one of myself with my aunt. Sometimes I pretend it's my mom, that she lived to see me graduate and join the Union fleet. I don't think she would've been as proud as my dad. But I can pretend. "It was a long time ago."

I shovel tofu loaf into my mouth. It doesn't taste as good as the pasta. "What else did he find?" I ask.

The captain stops at the window. We've passed most of the inner planets now, only a few of the outer giants to go until we reach Pluto and the *Posterus*. She looks lost and lonely staring out into space, with one side of her face dark and the other lit by the lights in my cabin.

"Dr. Prashad thinks it was implanted for one particular

purpose. We're not sure what that is yet, but I think it has something to do with Hartley. Also, he thinks it's…helped by sleep. Since you haven't been sleeping properly in the last few weeks, it hasn't been able to take control."

"What about the memory gaps? What does he think those are?"

She shrugs and leans against the shelf facing me. "You're going to have to ask him that."

"So if I don't sleep, it won't be able to control me?"

Her hands grip the edge of my shelf, and she sighs. "Ash, that's not what we're saying. You can't not sleep for the rest of your life."

"I can try."

She smirks. "Don't make me assign you a night guard. The way things are going now, I can't guarantee your safety." She pauses, like she's going to say something else, and I wish for a second she'd volunteer. I turn back to my food before she can see my blush.

When her silence continues, I turn back.

"Listen, Ash. I think there's something we need to address." She sighs and looks away from me. "I know you think I'm being hard on you. Maybe harder than I am on other crew. But I'm just trying to keep you safe." Her hands slide along the edge of my shelves, alternatively gripping and releasing. The nervous movement belies what she's not saying: She wants to keep everyone else safe.

And I want that, too.

"When I was younger, I used to dream about commanding my own ship. I had all these ideas about what it would be like—what I would be like as a captain…" She turns back to the window, her expression set in contemplation and her mind a million miles away. It's times like this I wish we weren't separated by rank. Because more than anything, I want to keep her safe.

"Sometimes the reality is harder than it looks, huh?"

After a moment, she clears her throat and pushes on as if the last conversation never happened. "How's your hip?"

"I'll have a bitchin' scar." I'm only half done with my meal, but I push it aside and reach for the chocolate pudding. I don't want to fill up before I get to the good part.

"Be serious, Ash. I need to know if you're okay to work, especially with the pace you keep." I turn to see she's taken a seat on my bed, legs crossed, leaning back on her arms like this is a casual chat between friends.

"It's fine, nothing a little time and distraction won't take care of."

The captain pulls a small syringe from her pocket. "I'm going to insert a tracker. It's just a precaution."

I lean back, arms folded. All the excitement of resuming my duties dies. It must be all over my face, because she reiterates the precaution part.

"I trust you. I do. This is for…" She turns the syringe in her hand, staring at it, not me. It's like she's two different people. When she's Jordan, she's confident and sure enough to joke and, dare I think, flirt. But every now and then, out comes another version. The one who hides behind her rank. I don't like this version of her so much. She's closed off and uptight.

"For everyone else," I say. They're going to track me like a criminal, make sure I don't go anywhere I'm not supposed to. And I can't say no, or I'll be stuck here.

When she does finally look at me, I can't read her expression. Is she ashamed? Maybe embarrassed? "This is my first command, and I'm still getting used to everything that means. When you become captain, there are certain sacrifices you make."

"That sounds like a tattoo the fleet commanders had you branded with."

Her face brightens, like she's going to laugh. It's unguarded but brief; all too soon it darkens. "Cara said something similar once."

"Who's Cara?"

She doesn't say anything. I can tell she's debating whether to tell me. I know it's inappropriate to be this familiar with my commanding officer. Maybe she feels the same crack in the barrier I do. It's as if that one simple act of compassion, placing her hand on my chest to comfort me, has tethered us.

"She was…we were engaged. And when she decided she didn't want to spend the rest of her life on a ship, we broke it off."

"She didn't want to come on the mission?"

She nods. "I keep thinking, how much did I actually love her if I wasn't willing to stay?"

I sit down next to her on the bed. There's a smudge of grease on the shoulder of her uniform. It looks new. It makes me wonder what she would be doing that involves grease. "How much did she love you if she wasn't willing to go?"

There's a pause where she stares at me and I stare at the grease.

I undo the first two buttons of my tunic and offer her my neck. There's a quick bite as she inserts the syringe.

"Are you sure I can't work two shifts? I'll be up anyway."

"Ash, why do you make everything so complicated?"

I shrug and smile. I've been asked this before. I don't set out to be difficult, but asking me to change is almost like asking an apple not to be an apple.

Chapter Ten

Don't disconnect them! Guys, how many times have I told you, if you use a dampener, you can reset the sheets for matter dispersion without having to go through the stupid re-initialization sequence. My way is ten times faster than yours."

I hear Hartley's voice booming through the engine room before I'm even halfway down the ladder. I'm amazed all over again when I step through the door. The room is cavernous and oddly silent. In my imagination, there should be giant combines thrashing up and down, propelling us through space. Instead, there are banks of floor-to-ceiling computers, black and shiny, reflecting back at each other.

"Ash!" Hartley yells from the back of the room. It echoes faintly before reaching me. "I heard you were back on active duty. How're you feeling?" He stands alone behind a workstation covered in what looks like little electronic pucks and various instruments in different stages of disassembly. His engine geeks must have scuttled off to find a dampener.

I snort because I have no idea how to answer. "I should be asking you that."

He waves me off. "I didn't have a diagnostic cube jammed in me while I was still conscious. Those things are brutal. Look!" He lifts his shirt as he's talking and points to a spot on his lower back. There's a red welt about ten centimeters long. "We have matching scars now." He says it like we've been marked for some secret club, as if seeing this identifying mark will prompt a highly evolved handshake or tell the other that we like pillow fights and sheet forts.

I walk over to get a closer look. "God, Hartley, is that what I did to you?" It's even worse up close. "I'm so sorry."

He flips his shirt back down and turns. He's got a look on his face as if I'm crazy. "Why are you sorry? It's not like you meant to stab me."

"I stabbed you?" Where the hell did I get a knife?

"Yeah, with a knife from the mess. It wasn't very deep, but the doc wanted to stitch it up anyway, just in case. I was in and out, so don't even worry about it. I think you got it worse. You look like grade A shit, Ash." He grins so big, you'd think that was a compliment.

"Thanks." I thought I'd ditched the hangover look. I run my hands down the front of my uniform. It's clean and pressed. I've showered about a million times. I tried to go for a run, but my hip still hurts too much, so I'm only 86 percent back to normal.

I don't even have to prompt Hartley. He's yammering as soon as he catches his breath. "You jumped me from behind. I felt this pinch, and when I turned, you'd already taken off down the hall. Security tried to take you down outside the airlock. You knocked 'em around pretty good, I heard." I wonder if he ever learned to breathe while talking, or if he always saves it all up for when he's done.

I reach for one of the small discs. They're a smooth cobalt on one side, tapered at the edges, and a dark metal on the other. Hartley screeches at me to leave those alone. My hand freezes a centimeter from one.

"What are they?"

"I call them Jackies." He grins wide, showing rows of white teeth. I know he wants me to ask him why, so I do. "Because they'll give you a coronary if you touch them in the wrong spot. Just like my ex, Jacki."

"You had a girlfriend?" I can't help the incredulous tone that creeps into my voice.

He ignores me and slips on a glove and picks one up and shows me the sides. With a soft hiss, the disc opens, revealing a bluish-white stream of light undulating around the circumference. "There's a current that will shoot one hundred amps into your body if it connects with flesh."

Jesus. "What possible use could you have for these?"

"These? Nothing. I adapted them from a failsafe we use on the engine bots. Sometimes the bots stop responding to our commands, which can be dangerous if they start wandering where they shouldn't. So, we have a smaller version of these"—he wiggles the disc—"attached to their motherboard. It uses a different frequency so we can overload the bot and stop them from damaging the engine."

I must have the look of death on my face because he grins wider and says: "Don't worry, Lieutenant. I only work on them during my own time, when I'm not sweating my balls off to get your projects done."

"Lieutenant Ash!" Two security guards and Corporal Vasa stand at the door. The guards even have weapons drawn. Hartley and I exchange a confused look, and then I remember the tracker.

"Oh. I guess you must be off-limits." I point to my neck, even though the tracker has now spread throughout my bloodstream, and explain, "I have a tracker."

He laughs. It's thunderous, and echoes throughout the spacious room. "If they frisk you, can I watch?"

"Are you all right, Hartley?" I'm not sure why Vasa's here, but I'm glad. I know he's less likely to let it get out of control.

"Guys, I'm fine. The lieutenant here just came by to ask if I wanted to go for lunch. She was just about to offer me her dessert as an apology for stabbing me." He wiggles his eyebrows at me. I roll my eyes in response.

"Was the armed escort necessary?" I ask.

"Sorry, Lieutenant." Vasa shifts back and forth on the balls of his feet. His wavy brown hair is stuck to his forehead with sweat. Every few seconds he runs his hands down his tunic, either to wipe the moisture from his hands or to make sure the front of his uniform is smooth. I notice he does this a lot. "The captain asked that I keep an eye on your whereabouts. She gave me a list." He points to Hartley. "He was on it. I may have overreacted." He turns to the guards and dismisses them.

"Keep an eye on me, yes, not come at me with guns." I want to know who else is on this list. If I have to worry about armed guards popping up every five minutes, I want fair warning. "You can run down the list over lunch. I apparently owe Hartley my chocolate pudding."

When we enter the mess, there are only a scattering of people, most of them too busy stuffing their faces to notice us. I recognize the glazed eyes and blank stares of the night shift. No outward signs of hostility yet. I admit, I'm using Hartley as a shield. I'm working on the theory that if Hartley can forgive me, and the crew sees, then they will be more likely to as well.

Once seated with our trays, I get Vasa to go over the captain's mandate again. It's hard to work up an appetite sitting across from him. He smells as if he showers with used socks and disinfectant. Part of it is his natural smell, which he's been written up for twice, and the other, his attempt at correcting that innateness.

"It's not as draconian as it sounds. The captain just gave me a list of places you wouldn't normally have cause to visit in the course of your duty. She's hoping if you are taken over by the mind knot, then we can catch it sooner. The list of places isn't that long, actually," says Vasa over a plate of tofu shaped to look like a pork chop without the chop or the pork. "It's mostly areas of the ship. The engine room, airlocks, the docking bay, other crew members' cabins—"

"Wait, I'm not allowed in other people's cabins?" What if there's a poker game? Half the fun of working on a ship is the after-hours games. And if you're good at them, they're a great way to augment your salary.

He shrugs and spears a tofu chop. "It's what's on the list. Ask the captain." The mess is filling up. A few people stop when they spot me, but most continue on.

"Anywhere else?"

"Yeah. Escape pods, you can't go near those, and for obvious reasons, weapons locker." A few people are openly gaping now, although it's not with the hostility I was expecting. Then I remember something Hartley said before, and I get a little worried.

"Hartley, how did you know I was awake when they inserted the diagnostic cube?"

His fork pauses halfway to his mouth, and I can see his brain working through the chain of people who told him. I eye my chocolate pudding. It will be warm by the time he gets to it, such a waste. Finally, he says, "I don't remember."

"It was probably Chloe. I heard she was pretty freaked out about the whole thing," says Vasa, reaching for his own chocolate pudding. "She kept telling everyone you were sent by the Burrs to blow up the ship." He shovels a huge spoonful in his mouth, and I turn away to stop from salivating and catch the table next to us listening to everything we say.

"Grab it to go, Vasa," I say as I pick up my tray. "Sorry, Hartley. I've got to get back to work, and, Vasa, you're coming with me."

I steer Vasa toward the bridge. I want to find out just how broad his mandate is. My guess is it involves more than babysitting.

The corridors are dead. Almost everyone is either on shift,

sleeping, or in the mess. Our boots click on the floors, like halting Morse code. "So, what else?" I ask when we get to the first chute to the next deck. "What other stuff does she have you working on?"

"Why should I tell you?"

"Why shouldn't you? Did she ask you not to?"

He shakes his head.

I give him my best hard-ass stare, perfected from hours of standing in front of a mirror, preparing for confrontations with my father. We stand like that for two minutes while he debates his options. I'm still his superior officer, and if the captain didn't give a direct order for me not to know, he doesn't have a good reason not to tell me. Even though, in all honesty, he knows he shouldn't. He's not stupid.

The smell wafting off his body is causing my sinuses to clog in self-defense. I hope he decides soon.

"Okay, fine," he says. Finally. I motion him up the ladder. I don't really want to go behind, but I have a thing about letting people climb up after me.

As he climbs, he talks. "She had me hack into the Europa SS database and check the timestamp of the security cameras during the attack with the reported arrival of the first ship."

"Why'd she do that? The first ship only took half a day." That's what they told me when I woke up on Alpha.

"That's what they thought. But the original timestamp was erased and replaced." He steps on the first deck and waits for me to join him on the landing.

"So if it was erased, how did you find it?"

"I know where to look?" He shrugs like it's no big deal, and I worry that there's a more significant revelation coming.

I stare pointedly at him.

"How long did it take?" I ask.

"Two weeks."

Two weeks! And she was going to keep this from me? "Wait.

So what happened to those two weeks?" My stomach knots. Two weeks, and yet somehow I still had a fresh wound in my back. The fact that they hacked the amount of time tells me the Burrs have something to hide. But worse, that's a lot of time spent on our space station with access to our people, our databases, and our technology.

I stare at Vasa's boots, which are shiny only on the very tip and dull everywhere else. The Burrs were on board the science station for those two weeks. Two weeks doing what?

Chapter Eleven

Maybe I should be grateful that I don't remember those two weeks. It's not like I sat and had tea every afternoon, and joined them for cocktails and after-dinner toddies or anything. I try and fail to think of what they would need all that time for. The mind knot wouldn't be all that difficult to install. The Burrs would have inserted it through my wound, and it would've propelled itself to my brainstem, then latched itself there like a parasite. If the Burrs actually were hiding on Europa station for two solid weeks, it could only be to steal crucial information from it, and its crew.

I think about it all through my duty shift and all through my hard-won second shift.

By dinner, I'm standing in the med center.

Dr. Prashad scolds one of the cooks while he stitches the cook's index finger on. It's been sliced between the first joint and the knuckle. Clearly, it's not the first time this has happened to him. I stand and observe, my hip thrumming with each prick and tug of the needle.

He glances up at me. "Be with you in a minute, Lieutenant," he says, without pausing his work.

I take a seat on one of the benches in the corner. The display above me is a looped video of the inside of someone's esophagus swallowing food that looks very much like what I had for lunch—after I've chewed it. We travel with the food down the esophagus, into the stomach, where the food sits and sinks for what feels like a few seconds, but because the video's been sped up, is probably more like an hour. We continue our journey into the small intestines, and then the large. I stop watching after that.

Jesus. Who picks this stuff as waiting room entertainment? I have an idea it's the doctor. One of those folks who is very appreciative of medicine as art. Like those people who have photographs of microscopic cells on their walls behind their desk, picked because they're colorful and pretty, yet really are some deadly virus.

At last, my wait is over. We finally get around to the exam and why I'm there, and Dr. Prashad's face lights up as if I've just become his weekend fix-it project.

"I don't know how much I can help you, but I'll try." His hand lingers on my arm for a moment, in comfort from my earlier experience, or excitement at a new challenge, I'm not sure.

He pulls up an image of my brain on the monitor beside us and points to a region of my brain. "See right here, that part shaped like a seahorse? That's your hippocampus. It's where you store your long-term memories." He swipes his hand, and a new image comes up.

At first, I can't tell what it is, then I notice the tentacles and realize it's my new housemate, the mind knot the Burrs left as their calling card. They're wafting, and as they undulate, tiny particles fall away or are secreted and drift upward.

"The mind knot is releasing a chemical, this stuff right here, and it's getting sucked up into your bloodstream. As far as I can tell, it's inhibiting parts of your hippocampus."

"Can you reverse it?"

"Not yet. But there might be another way in." He opens a drawer and takes out a few vials and sets them on the counter in front of him. "The chemical the mind knot is releasing into your bloodstream hasn't erased your memories, just suppressed them. If I can find the right mix, I may be able to help you get past the blockage." He takes the vials over to a white box with holes in top, inserts an empty vial, and slips each glass tube into a slot on top. "I'm going to try to suppress whatever is stopping you from accessing those memories. It's like temporarily raising a gate so you can enter a blocked area."

"Will I just instantly remember everything?" I wonder if it would be similar to waking up with foggy bits of memory after too much drinking the night before.

He pops out the now-full vial and slips it into a syringe. "To be honest, I'm not sure how this will work exactly. But I'm reasonably sure it won't kill you."

Oh, joy.

I pull my tunic on because it's suddenly freezing in here.

The doctor reaches out to pull my collar down, and I back up. "Wait. You want to do this now?"

"Do you have somewhere else to be?"

My stomach grumbles in response to that. I'm really wishing I hadn't skipped dinner before coming. But more importantly, what if I never wake up? What if this makes the effects of the mind knot worse? But instead of protesting, I shake my head. I need to know what happened on Europa.

"I didn't think so." He sticks the needle deep into my skin and presses the plunger. It takes a second to kick in, but when it does, my vision goes white, then red, then dark.

When I wake, I'm standing in the lab on the Europa Science Station, staring out at the stars. It's weird because everything is hyper-real, as if I'm actually standing looking out the window as we orbit Jupiter's moon Europa and beyond that, Jupiter itself. I have no control over my movements at all. I know this because I pick up a mug and drink from it. From its chips and cracks and faded slogan—"World's Worst Cousin" printed in bold capital letters—I recognize it as the mug Edward gave me for my twenty-first birthday.

And then the world explodes.

My head and neck slam forward and the rest of me crashes backward. When I've stopped moving, I look down at my hands—which are covered in blood—and I feel something digging into me from behind. I remember, but it's an odd out-of-body memory because I've seen it before on the security camera. I want to look around for the camera, but all I can do is stare at my hands, confused by the blood and glass and how it got there.

Smoke billows in through the door, and I pull myself free after three or four good heaves. I collapse on the floor, coughing and retching from smoke. It's not smoke from the explosion. They've released tiny canisters throughout the deck, spewing foul, black smoke. But this revelation comes too late, as one sails toward me, bounces off my knee, and whirls away into the darkness before popping. Everything goes black.

I wake up groggy. For a second I think I'm back in the med center with one hell of a hangover, but when I try to move, I am still stuck inside myself, experiencing what must be my lost memories.

My wrists are strapped tight to a chair. The cord cuts into my skin. My ankles are also bound, and for some terrifying reason, the Burrs have removed my boots and socks.

This doesn't look like any part of the station. The floors are caked in so much grease that they're black, even though I can tell from the corners that the tiles were once white. I'm aboard one of their ships.

I can see and feel everything but have no guard against it, no mechanism to escape. As if being paralyzed while Pomeranians lunch on my innards. I feel tired and weak. The drug they gave me must not have worn off yet. Too heavy to hold up any longer, my head lolls onto my chest, and every few seconds I hear a sound. *Pit, pat, pit, pat.* After a few minutes, I notice it's me making that sound, or rather the blood dripping off my face onto my pants.

Boots stop a foot from my bare feet. They're so worn that I can see the metal tips poking through the material on top. This close, I can smell him. It's a mixture of fish and dung and soil. I still don't raise my head. It'll take too much energy, and I know I don't have any to spare if I'm going to survive this. I'm scared. No, scared isn't the right word, neither is terrified. It's an equal mixture of morbid fascination—to see what they're going to do—and fatalistic anticipation—because I know something is coming. I'm just not sure what.

I feel fingers dig and twist into my hair and wrench my head up. I'm staring into the face of my enemy. It's pocked with craters, and the skin around his eyes looks like it's slipped out of place, revealing too much of his eyeball and socket. But he's human, not monster. Then again, I've seen a Burr before, just not this close. Monster is a relative term. He grins. It's mostly gums, with the odd tooth poking through. I guess they don't have much of a dental plan.

Thanks to the shift in gravity, blood from my nose begins to dribble down my lips. I choke as it slips into my mouth and down my throat. It splatters across his face. He slams my head back into the headrest. I feel it in my teeth.

While my teeth settle back into their sockets, someone new enters the room. This one is different. His black hair—which I can tell is dyed because it's so uniform—is slicked back. It's stark against his pale skin, and his eyes are so blue, it's like someone painted globs of blue paint on either side of his nose. His skin isn't smooth, but it's not wrinkled either, as if it was pulled taut and tucked around his hairline. It's unsettling because he was once handsome but now looks as if he's been repaired too often.

This is the guy in charge. Four-Teeth drops my head, but I manage to keep it up and continue to stare. I hope my expression says *go fuck yourself*, although I suspect, because of the bloody nose and general dishevelment, it says *If I don't sleep soon, I'll pass out.*

He opens a panel beside the door and enters a sequence of commands. The chair begins to tilt back. The armrests shift to pull my arms down flat beside me, and the bottom of the chair swings up so that my legs are flat with the rest of my body.

"Go wash up," Stretched-Face says to Four-Teeth, who scurries off, which I don't see because I'm now lying on my back facing the ceiling. "Alison…" His voice is deep and gravelly, like it's an engine starting deep in his throat before it barrels out of his mouth. He steps over to a cabinet hidden in the wall and pulls out a long, thin rod. My eyes follow it, and not him, as he moves to stand over me at the head of the bed.

He holds the crop up to the light, examining it, almost as if he's forgotten that I'm lying on the table. "It's interesting, don't you think? Of all the things we've invented, we always come back to the basics." He swishes the rod downward. It makes a whooshing sound as it moves through the air. "For instance, I could use a variety of advanced technologies to get what I need from you, Alison, but instead I'm going to use this." He holds the rod closer to my face. "A riding crop used to discipline horses." The skin on his face has barely moved as he's said this. "I sometimes think we as a species don't appreciate the simple. We complicate things. Take you, for example." He places the rod on the side of my face and turns it toward him. His blue eyes bore into mine. "You know something I want to know."

I try to shake my head, but the rod stays firm. My chest is tight, and I just want the pain to start so it can be over that much sooner.

"This station is working on a plasma pulse, is that correct?"

I don't say anything. I have no idea what he's talking about, but that doesn't mean the *me* who experienced this didn't. He lifts the rod, and before I even have time to brace for it, he whips the table next to my head. I flinch at the sharp slap next to my ear. I clench my fists and teeth. There's something very much like panic building inside me. The longer he holds off, the worse I feel.

"The plasma pulse is a device used to disrupt the engines and electrical current of a ship," he says, playfully bending the rod back and forth. My lips are squeezed tight. My teeth dig in, but it's a pain I can endure. He strikes the table again. Harder. This time near my right ear. This isn't panic I'm feeling any longer, it's pure anger. I want him to stop stalling; it's almost worse than if he were actually whipping me.

"It's very simple, Lieutenant. You know the passcodes to get me this device, and I have food and water and a nice cot when you do."

I stare up at him and smile. "You're right. It is simple. I'd rather the rod than tell you anything."

His jaw clenches. It's the first expression I've seen him make. Fury. His brows climb while the rest of his face tightens toward the center.

He pulls his arm back and this time whips my left arch so hard it feels like a hot knife has sliced through the soft skin of my foot.

CHAPTER TWELVE

I wake screaming. My body is throbbing as if I've had a dream I couldn't wake from. My stomach curls, and I dry heave, retching over the side of the bed. Dr. Prashad is at my side in a second, rubbing my back. He watches me with concern. The skin between his eyebrows bulges. I open my mouth to tell him I'm fine, but bile rises, and I spit green slime into the kidney-shaped container he's shoved under my face.

After a minute or two, I lean back on the bed. The muscles in my stomach have settled, and I feel a little better.

"What?" I ask.

It's an intense stare now. "I was worried. Your heart rate was…"

We both look over at the monitor and see the peak, a Mount Everest next to a series of hills.

"Did the serum work?"

I nod. "It worked." A little too well, I think. I wonder if he knows that by giving me back those memories, he's triggered others. I can remember the plasma pulse. It's why I was assigned there in the first place, to oversee the final stages of its development. I need to know if I gave them any information, if the Burrs now have the plasma pulse, and if they do, what they're planning on doing with it. I need more answers, more of my memories back.

I grab the doctor's sleeve. "I need to go again."

He laughs and unfolds my hand from his sleeve. "Not tonight. You need sleep and a decent meal."

I want to argue. I need to know more right now, but the doctor is almost as stubborn as me. It's an argument I'll lose.

My first thought is of the captain. I know it's irrational to be so drawn to her. Yet just being in her presence calms me. I should tell her what's happened, and I jump off the bed with that in mind. Before I've buttoned my tunic, I stop, my mind changed. What do I tell her? That I might have given those assholes technology that can cripple us? Because what do I really know? The rational side of me wins, and I decide to wait until I find out more. But it doesn't stop the ache that's begun building in my chest. The longing.

Later, as I sit in the middle of my duvet in bed clothes, I pull first one foot up, then the other. I can't see any marks. But then, there wouldn't be. He probably couldn't risk any suspicion that I'd experienced more than an explosion. I run my fingers over the smooth, pinkish skin. I was right. It wasn't such a bad thing, not remembering what had been done.

I was told the Burrs had attacked for food and medical supplies. But they hadn't. They were there to steal the schematics for the plasma pulse, and if they got them, they probably erased any evidence of the theft.

I lie back, hands laced behind my head, and for the fourth night in a row, I don't sleep well. When I do, my dreams are full of Burrs, and blue eyes, and horses with large black rods, and for some reason, bright green pears.

The next afternoon, I'm in the bow of the ship. The tight compartment houses the ship's sails for matter collection and several banks of filters. I'm sitting cross-legged on the floor with tools and filters scattered around me in a semicircle, and for the first time in days, I'm happy, lost in busywork that allows me to think. As first officer, there are more important things I should be doing, but I hate officers who refuse to get their hands dirty, and there's something comforting about being holed up with a labor-intensive task ahead of me.

All four hundred and ninety filters have to be fitted with sensors, ones that detect photons with short wavelengths. Anything with a kinetic energy greater than one multiplied by ten to the power of eighteen eV could be lethal over time. When the filters detect harmful wavelengths, an alarm is tripped, and our artificial electromagnetic field is activated to protect the crew and ship from the adverse effects. The way the *Persephone* is set up now, the ship's artificial electromagnetic field is always activated, but that's a huge drain on resources. It's important when we're in our solar system, so close to the sun and its devastating solar wind, but as we move farther away, we won't need it to be on constantly. Our biggest worry, as we move farther from the Milky Way, is gamma ray bursts from supernovas, exploding stars, or the fusion of two neutron stars. The amount of kinetic energy produced by gamma rays puts the energy output of our sun to shame. Without this protection, we would be subjected to lethal doses of radiation.

Much like the Earth's magnetospheres, our shield separates out the protons and electrons from the solar wind, which in turn generates a separation of charge in space and deflects the particles from space. Basically, it's a generator that creates static electricity to push harmful rays away from us.

I begin my task thinking how simple life must have been on Earth—it naturally produces its own electromagnetic field to shield the planet from harmful space radiation—when I hear a whoosh, and the locking clamp on the compartment door slides into place. I rush to the door, but it's locked from the outside. I crane to see through the glass, to see who is on the other side. No one. I turn around to search for what, I'm not sure. Nothing will pry these doors open. They're designed to be airtight in case of a breach in the hull. And then I hear another sound, much more dangerous than the first.

I rush to one of the sealed airways and place my ear against it. There's a faint sound, like sucking air through your nose, and when I put my hand next to the flue, I can feel the draw. Someone is decompressing this compartment. I have at most five minutes before all the oxygen is siphoned and this room will be a vacuum—no air, just space.

I search the room for another panel with an override command to reinitialize compression. I notice one near the door, but when I try to open it, the damn thing won't budge. I run my fingers along the edge looking for any give, but it's been soldered shut. I grab a hammer and screwdriver from my pile of tools in the middle of the room and begin to beat the screwdriver into the edge of the panel, to use it as a crowbar to pry the door open. Nothing. It's not even making a dent in the solder. I throw the screwdriver on the ground and chuck the hammer at the door in frustration.

Is it my imagination? Or is the air getting thinner? I undo the first three buttons on the collar of my tunic. The air has become humid, and I'm finding it harder to keep my focus. I stare out of the tiny porthole at the very bow of the ship. Beyond, I can see a mass of stars. Usually, the only thing you see is the back of the sails, but they're currently furled. I focus on the stars, calming my mind. If I panic, I'll die. I need to use my brain. *Every situation has a solution.*

I take a closer look at the panel. I run my finger down the side and realize it hasn't been soldered. It was welded. We don't even allow welding tools to be used on board; the only place they're allowed is outside the ship, during spacewalks. Welding requires sparks, and that's too dangerous to have in such an oxygen-rich environment. Too many things could go wrong. Two things pop into my mind. One, someone with access to the welding gear did this, and two, whoever it was went to a lot of trouble.

There must be another way into that panel. I take stock of the tools I have with me: four hundred and ninety sensors, a hammer, screwdriver, pliers, and an Allen wrench. Excellent! Everything I need to die a slow painful death of oxygen deprivation. I scan the room for anything that might be useful. It's only two and a half meters wide, and one and a half long, and besides the filter banks, there isn't anything else in the room.

I search the walls, running my hands up and down. My fingers skim over a slight seam, and that's when I notice the strips of paneling. I grab the screwdriver and begin to inch it along the seam, prying it up. When I have enough of it up to slip the screwdriver in, I take the hammer and strike the back of the screwdriver, then place it behind to use as a lever. After a minute, I have enough of a section to get my hand inside and pull it out. I grip tight and wrench.

It's not until I have enough of a section exposed that I realize my hands are covered in blood. My palms have been sliced open from the sharp metal of the paneling. I wipe them on my pants and squeeze my shoulder and arm into the opening, trying to reach the compression control panel from behind.

I wish I'd brought a flashlight. I feel my way to the back of the panel, searching for the wire that connects to the override switch. Something bites into my skin. I pull my hand out and suck on my finger. I breathe in through my nose and out through my mouth. It's getting harder to think. I can do this. I have to be careful where I touch, or I'll get another shock. It's just like the animal pens back on Alpha. I see Edward's mocking face, egging me on. I can do this.

I worm my hand through the wires and cables, using memory to trace which wire does what. I lean my head against the wall. It's easier to hold myself up this way. My muscles ache from the effort of standing. I breathe in through my nose and hold it for a second. I think I have it. Another piercing shock runs through my hand, and I pull it out.

Panic wells up inside me. It's so fierce, my vision blurs, and a thought comes into my head. I remember this feeling. I've experienced this before. My breathing speeds up. I'm terrified and hyperventilating, and even as I can rationally put a name to what's happening to me, I'm unable to use that same rationale to stop it. I sink to the floor on all fours, trying to pull air into my lungs, but it's too fast. Without even realizing how or when, I'm curled up on the floor with my knees tucked into my chest. I need to get up. I need to pull air into my lungs, but don't feel I can do both at once. My eyes close, and the last thing I see is dark blue eyes.

Chapter Thirteen

The first thing I see is Vasa and two security guards standing over me.

At last, he says, "What the hell happened?"

"Someone locked me in and decompressed the room."

"Why didn't you recompress it?" Vasa walks over to the panel and tries to open it. "Oh," he says when he can't.

I can tell from his face when the scene in front of him begins to make sense. He turns to the guards and tells them to get the captain.

I don't want her to see me like this, like a cat who shit itself because it got trapped in a box. "I'm fine. Don't bring her into this."

He kneels down in front of me and helps me sit up. "Ash, you're covered in blood. One or maybe several of the crew just tried to kill you. She's gonna want to know. You didn't think the tracker was just for the crew's protection, did you?" Vasa's dirty-sock stench fills my nostrils, but I don't even mind. Anything familiar is comforting right now.

It doesn't take long for the captain to get there. She must have run most of the way because the guards are a few minutes behind her. She stops dead at the door, slightly out of breath, a few strands of inky hair out of place, and takes in the room. When our eyes lock, her shoulders relax.

"Jesus, Ash. They told me there was an accident."

Vasa helps me to stand. "It wasn't an accident," he says. "I'm going to let Ash tell you what happened. We're waiting on a message from the *Posterus*, and if I'm not there to intercept it, we'll have to wait a full twelve hours before they can resend." He gives me a pointed look before withdrawing with the guards.

I should be thankful. If the captain hadn't insisted on the tracker and ordered Vasa to keep an eye on me, I'd be dead. But I'm not. I'm furious, and I'm not sure if it's at her or myself for needing the help in the first place.

She lifts my chin, inspecting my neck and face. Her eyes shift to the pried paneling and then widen. Seeing it from her perspective, I feel even more embarrassed.

She grabs for one of my hands. Turning it over, she lifts it to examine the damage. The cuts on my palms have clotted. It looks worse than it really is. It doesn't even hurt that much. I close my eyes, fighting a mixture of emotions. I feel the panic rising again, but I'd rather the anger instead.

"What happened?"

I shrug and open my eyes. She's staring straight into them, and my breath catches at the closeness and intensity.

"I got locked in, and the room began decompressing."

She does the same thing Vasa did, she checks the panel next to the door, and when it doesn't open, she leans in close to inspect it.

"It's welded," she says in shock.

I nod.

Her brain is working through the sequence, seeing the filters and tools spread around the room. She looks back at me and just stares. After a moment, just when I think she's going to turn and leave, she smacks the wall with her palm.

"What the hell were you doing working in here alone? Haven't you been paying attention?" She kicks a filter sensor across the room, and it splinters against the far wall. "Of course not, because you just do what you want to do, Ash, without thinking of anyone but yourself. You're goddamned reckless." It's a flash of anger so surprising and unexpected from the usually calm captain that my heart constricts.

Her anger is gone in an instant, replaced by her regular mask.

She's right. I have been reckless. I thought because Hartley had forgiven me, the rest of the crew would as well. But the hate and prejudice are too much for some to get over. Chloe's fears have worked their way through the ship and taken hold. "I'm relieving you of duty, Ash. Effective immediately."

I clamp my eyes shut to stop the tears. It would be a second death to cry in front of a commanding officer, the first of course being dumb enough to sleep with one. "Why? It's not my fault. This isn't my fault. Why are you punishing me?" I hate the pleading in my voice. "Please don't relieve me of duty. You're just letting them win if you do that. They'll think you're siding with them."

"Good!" She grips my arm. Her fingernails dig into my skin. Her eyes glare into mine as if she's trying desperately to make me understand. "I want them to think that. I have a crew that's mutinied." She nods at my shocked expression. "Yes, that's what you call it when a crew turns against its superior officers. And I have to squash it as fast as possible. I can't let them win, or I'll lose all credibility as a captain. I need to remove you from the situation." She drops my arm. "I need you safe," she says as she turns and walks out of the room.

I wait only thirty seconds before rushing after her. I'm not some mindless bot being controlled by the enemy. I can fight against it. I know I can.

I find her at the ladder about to climb up to the next deck and grab her arm. I spin her to face me. "Would you relieve any other member of the crew if they were in this situation and not me?" I have no idea what's possessed me to do this. I've never questioned a commanding officer before.

She pulls me out into the corridor and waves her hand to close the door, afraid the sound of our argument will travel up the chute. “Of course I would.” Her nostrils flare with each breath she takes. She’s still mad as hell.

I don’t believe her. She’s afraid of me, afraid I’ll come under control of my mind knot, just like the rest of the crew. How do I make her believe that I won’t lose control? “Bullshit!” I shout. “Hartley was back on duty the next day. You haven’t treated him like a pariah.” This is almost like being back on Europa, experiencing my memories and not being able to control myself. I have the rationale to see the trouble ahead, but no power to stop it from happening.

Her cheeks are flushed, two round blooms of pink, on either side of her otherwise pale face. Her breathing has slowed, but only just. She’s trying to remain calm, but everything tells me she’s barely holding herself in check. Her grip on my arm gets tighter. “Is that what you think I’m doing?”

“Yes! I’m not going to go ballistic on the crew. I can control this. I’m not some child. I can take care of myself.” The more I say it, the more I can believe it’s true. If I dwell on what-ifs, I’ll go insane. I jerk my arm free and stomp back to the compartment, aware as I do that I’m now acting like the child I claimed I wasn’t.

“Oh, Jesus, Ash. It’s precisely that kind of attitude that’s going to get you killed. I don’t expect anyone on my ship to have to be able to ‘take care of themselves.’ I want everyone to work together or not at all.” By the time she finishes, she’s at the door watching me clean the room.

I’m not even paying attention to what I’m doing, throwing tools into a pile, collecting sensors and dumping them into my tool case. I just need to do something, anything, to get my mind off this argument and calm down. The panic is there, lurking behind every action.

“I can’t do it,” I say. “I can’t sit and do nothing.” I turn to look at her, still standing at the threshold, gripping the doorjamb. "Captain, I'm afraid I'll go mad if I'm not working."

Her gaze shifts to look past me at the star field through the porthole. I wish I knew what she was thinking.

"Fine. One shift, and you can run your teams from the bridge." The bridge, where there'll be at least five babysitters if anything goes wrong.

"The bridge?" I'm about to protest more, but stop. I can see the rebuttal on her lips. I should be grateful she's given me this much. "Thank you, Captain."

She steps into the room and pulls me to my feet. "Ash, I want you to be careful. Don't trust anyone, including Hartley." She brushes my hair back off my shoulder, unaware she's doing it before it's done. Her arm slips away, and she backs up as if she doesn't want to be this close to me, and I notice the flush is back.

"Hartley?" She thinks Hartley could be behind this? "Are we talking about the same person? I don't believe that he could keep a secret if he tried."

"Maybe not, but remember, you did try to kill him."

I'm almost sure Hartley didn't do this, but the way she's carrying on, it's as if everyone's out to get me. "*I* didn't try to kill him. This thing in my head did."

"You're still not getting it, Ash. No one sees you anymore, all they see is the mind knot. As far as they're concerned, you're under the control of the Burrs. And at any moment, 'this thing,'" she taps the side of my temple, "could have you trying to kill one of them."

"Is that how you see me?"

"Of course not."

I want to ask how she sees me. Does she see me as a monster like the rest of the crew? Instead, I take a step toward her. I need to see her reaction. Is she afraid of me? She doesn't move. Her eyes search every inch of my face.

"Are you afraid I'm going to turn against the crew?" I ask.

Her eyes widen as I say this. "No, Ash," she whispers, "that's not what I'm afraid of," and takes the last step separating us. With only centimeters between us, every heat receptor in my body ignites. Is she proving she's not afraid?

This close, I'm rewarded with a hint of apricots. She runs a hand gently down my arm, and even though it's the lightest touch, it seeps through my uniform and into my skin. And I'm suddenly not worried about duty shifts or mind knots. But before I can react, she's gone.

CHAPTER FOURTEEN

It's late. I should be sleeping, as I had promised the doctor and the captain, but I can't get my mind to shut off. Someone wants me dead. Probably a bunch of someones. It's so surreal I can't wrap my head around the idea. It feels more like an apocryphal story Edward would tell us as kids.

So here I am, at zero three hundred hours, on the track, running my mind blank. It's the only thing that will make it settle. Sweat pooling and heart racing. Running is the only thing that tethers the demons.

I round the next bend, and before I can pull back, I crash into the captain, knocking us both to the ground.

I sit up too quick, and my head spins. The captain stares at me from the ground. I catch a trace of apricots. It's even more powerful than usual. For several moments neither of us move. We just stare, my heart drumming irregular beats.

"I'm sorry, Captain." I reach out a hand and help us stand. Her long fingers wrap around mine. They're comforting and strong, and it's with reluctance I let go. At this moment, I wish we could be on Alpha, and she was just someone I had met in a pub.

Her cheeks are flushed, and her sweater has fallen off her shoulder, revealing skin so pale I can see a hint of blue veins beneath. Her hair is pulled back into a messy ponytail.

Before I know what I'm doing, I reach up and tuck a stray tendril behind her ear. As my thumb brushes over her ear, her eyes close and breath catches, and I pull back aware, at that moment, of the consequences. Mortified, I take off sprinting. My legs and arms pump, moving around the track at an impossible speed. Running out my fears, my wants, my frustrations. She's gone by the time I finish my first lap.

After thirty minutes, my lungs are burning. My muscles are screaming, but I keep going. I can't stop, not until my mind does. I've never been so drawn to anyone. And I've never been so certain it's a want I can't have. Fraternizing with commanding officers is a short road to a court martial. It's always been a rule I've found easy to follow. But then my commanding officers have never been gorgeous young women.

After forty-five minutes, my legs give out, and I drop to the ground, gasping. My skin is slick with sweat, and my shirt is soaked. I push my forehead into the surface of the Tartan Track, bowing in supplication to some unknown force. My whole body is heaving. The stippled texture cuts into my forehead. I sit up before all my blood rushes to my head. The last thing I need is to faint and to be found passed out on the running track. I want to cry. I want to scream. I need some sort of release, and right now I don't care which. I use the railing to help me stand and trudge up one deck to wash it all away.

In the showers, I close my eyes. The steam forms droplets on my skin. The heat eases my burning muscles. Then suddenly, I'm turned and slammed against the tile wall. Through the blur of water, I see Jordan's dark hair slink down her back as the hot spray washes over her. Her mouth is on mine. Her naked body is pressed against mine, digging my shoulder blades into the cold tile. My mouth opens, and her tongue invades it. She reaches around my neck and pulls me closer.

I'm on fire.

My whole body has interrupted any conscious control and

just reacts to everything all at once. I feel her hand slide down to my breast. She cups it and kneads my nipple. The sensation races toward my groin. I moan. It starts deep in my throat and spreads throughout my whole body. My mind is everywhere at once trying to make sense of what's happening. I want to pull back, to catch my breath, but my hands betray me, and instead of pushing her back, they wrap themselves around her head and pull her closer.

I can feel her mouth curl in triumph. She takes my bottom lip between her teeth and bites, pulling it with her as she leans back. She lets go, and we stare at each other, panting, bodies touching. We stand like that until we've caught our breath. Tentatively she leans in and kisses my neck, running her fingers along my collarbone and down to my breasts. Her kisses follow. She takes a nipple into her mouth and sucks hard. My head falls back against the wall as she nips at it. She moves to the other. As she plays her tongue over it, her hands rove farther south, running along my hip bones and upper thighs.

I have never wanted anyone so much.

She pulls back, and her blue eyes dance in amusement as she lightly trails her tongue down my stomach, past my navel. Her hands run up my inner thighs, and as her tongue gently glides over my clit, I cry out. Her hands splay my legs as her tongue licks in rhythm with my heartbeat.

Everything I am at this moment is focused on that one spot. I want to slow it down and savor every moment of her raspy tongue. But I'm so close already. And then I feel her finger slip inside me. It curls in a come-hither movement, and I'm undone. I come loudly. My legs quiver as her tongue and finger continue around my moaning.

I slink to the floor beside her, breathing hard. For the first time in weeks, I don't feel the panic. I'm not thinking about anything, just her.

She sweeps her wet hair back. As she does, her breasts lift, and I'm reminded of a Greek sculpture that I once saw in a picture book, every muscle, and curve carved with care. The artist had loved the woman, but I wonder if he was in love with her or the ideal? Did he fall in love with what he'd created, or could he see the original within the ideal? I'm worried I'm making the same mistake. There's still so much I don't know about her. But it's too heavy a thought for this moment.

I reach out and brush my fingertips along her shoulder. They travel down past her full teardrop breasts, down her slender waist, down her muscular legs. Every inch of her is taut. She closes her eyes. Steam particles settle and pool on her body, forming rivulets that run between her breasts. They collect in her hair and on her lashes. I skim the backs of my fingers up her inner thighs, and they part for me.

Still, on the shower room floor, I lean in and graze my lips against hers. As I run my fingers lightly through her folds, my tongue and finger slip in at the same time. Her moan, when it reaches me through the haze, is throaty and deep. It makes me wet, and ready again in an instant.

I nudge her back to lean against the shower wall. Her legs fall open, welcoming me farther. Her heat envelops me and spreads through my body as if the connection fuses us together as one. Cupping the back of her head, I bring her closer, crushing our lips together. In this moment, I'm not thinking about my memory loss, about the Burrs or mind knots. For the first time in months, I'm focused on one thing, one goal. I need to hear and feel Jordan come around my fingers.

"Jordan," I breath against her lips.

She lets out a startled cry, and her eyes snap open. Pushing through the arousal is fear. She searches my face, as if I have all the answers, as if the curves and lines of my face can tell her how she ended up here. How she ended up naked on the floor of the communal shower in this compromising position.

She pushes me back and unfolds herself from the floor. “Alison, I…”

Jordan’s never called me by my first name before. She says it stiffly and it has the effect of dumping a bucket of cold water over my head. I start to shiver.

I reach up and turn off the water, and wish I hadn’t. There’s nothing left to fill the void. I pull myself up and back against the wall, pressing my palms to the cold tile. Instead of finding solid support, which should calm me, it just makes me colder, and I tremble even more.

“Ali…” She steps back and in that movement, I see everything she’s thinking. Everything she means to say is plain on her face: regret. I’m a regret. Her eyes squeeze shut, and all my attention is on her. Her full breasts rise and fall with her breath, her jaw tightens, and her frown lines deepen. Even though she hasn’t said a word, her body has said it all for her. This was a mistake.

But I want to hear her say it out loud. This silent rejection is worse than anything I have ever had to endure.

“What?” I laugh, but there’s no humor in it, and it melts on my lips and threatens to become a sob. What was I expecting? A declaration of love? I suck in a shaky breath and walk out of the shower.

Three weeks ago, I would never have imagined this moment in my life, and even now, as I’m in it, living it, surviving it, I still don’t believe it. What was I thinking?

I pull on pants and throw a shirt over my head. When I pull it down, Jordan is standing across from me, still not speaking, even though I can see she’s trying. Her face crumples in what can only be shame. She looks almost as if she finally got that gift she always dreamed of, but in less than five minutes of owning it, she discovers it wasn’t what she wanted.

That realization cuts straight through me. “I don’t get it,” I say as I stuff my running clothes into my bag. “I’ve had commanding officers make passes at me before—although not as successfully as yours. Was I supposed to push you away?"

She reaches for my hand but pulls back. She can't even look at me now. All her attention is focused on her fingers as she clenches them. "Ali."

I throw my bag down on the bench.

She flinches as if this is causing her physical pain.

"Stop saying that!" I yell. "Just stop—stop being such a coward and tell me. What was that?" I'm hurt. This hurts. It's like my heart has torn a hole and is seeping acid into my chest. The pain is worse than anything I've ever experienced before, and what's worse is I don't know why it should. Maybe it's just the look of rejection on her face.

"This shouldn't have happened," Jordan says.

We've only known each other a few weeks, and I know it's a mistake, but there's something about it that guts me. When she doesn't say anything more, I sling my bag over my shoulder and rush out of the change room.

Chapter Fifteen

I'm slumped on one of the beds in the med center and overwhelmed as Dr. Prashad bandages my hands. I can still feel Jordan's breath on me, hear her throaty moan in my ear, feel her heat on my fingers. These images pulse through my mind and other traitorous parts. I should be more worried about my possible assassins, but there are so many other things pushing and shoving around my mind, fighting to be heard.

We are both silent as he wraps my hands. Again. My extracurricular activities last night proved too much, and I woke with blood-soaked bandages. I've spent far too much time here since I reported for my medical three weeks ago.

After a more thorough exam than I think is necessary, I convince him to let me go under again. As he prepares the syringe, I grip the table so tight that I can feel it cutting into my shredded palms. Now that I know what I'm in for, it's not as easy to psych myself up. I lie back and stare at the exam lights above me. My heart is pounding against my rib cage, and I wonder if this is what Jordan meant when she said I was reckless. Is this even a good idea? But I don't have any more time to second-guess myself. I need more information about what the Burrs did on Europa station. The doctor moves my collar aside and sticks me with another syringe.

❖

I'm squatting on a grungy floor staring at my bare feet. My arms are tied behind my back with a plank of metal propping them up. It forces my torso forward, placing all my weight on my legs and feet, which are still sore from being whipped with the rod. The result is excruciating. By the severe ache in my legs and arms, I know I've been in this position for a long while. So long, in fact, that I've pissed myself. The dampness stretches from my crotch halfway down my leg. The smell of urine mixes with the stench from my body.

I wonder how long I've been here on their ship when I see a familiar pair of boots step into my field of vision. I know they belong to the man with the rod. He kneels in front of me and tilts my chin up so I'm staring into eager eyes. After a few seconds, I notice they have tiny flecks of turquoise and gray interwoven with the deep blue.

"Are we ready to talk, Alison?"

I try to pull away. Only my father calls me that. And now Jordan. He grips my chin with his fingernails, and they bite into my skin. I shake my head. Instead of his, I see Jordan's face in profile. I sink into the memory of her on the bridge, giving me a wink after Vasa's said something in twenty words that could've been said in three. It's not much, but it's enough to remember that this will end. This horror will be temporary.

"No?" He stalks over to a table in the far corner of the room. After a moment, I realize we're in his cabin. There isn't much to it, just a bed in the far corner, the sheets pulled tight from corner to corner, a washroom off to the side, and a desk clear of everything except one lonely tablet. When he turns back, he's carrying a ripe green pear he's picked from a small tree sitting under a heat lamp on the table. The pears glisten in the warm light, wet from the spray bottle next to the tree. Next to the bottle is a pair of pruning scissors and a collection of dead leaves. It's obvious this tree is loved.

"You must be starving." He sits down in front of me, crossing his legs, and pulls out a knife.

I flinch.

He smirks as he slices into the pear. "I'm not going to cut you, Alison." He pops the sliver of pear into his mouth and taps my knee with the blade of the knife. It brings my focus back to the pain lacing my thigh muscles. He cuts another piece. "Would you like some, Alison?" His voice is measured and calm, almost pleasant like we were out to dinner, and he's asking what I'd like from the wine menu.

I wish he'd stop calling me that. The way he keeps saying my name after each sentence, I think he's doing it on purpose, to get a rise out of me.

He holds the slice of pear out toward my mouth. I shake my head. I don't want anything from this man. Before I know what's happening, he pulls my hair, tilting my head back. My mouth opens involuntarily, and he places the pear on my tongue. It melts when I refuse to chew it. The sweet syrup slides down my throat. In the memory, I can feel myself getting ready to spit it back in his face, but some deep buried self-preservation instinct kicks in and overrides my stubbornness.

I swallow and stare.

He reaches behind me and pulls the metal plank out, releasing me from the stress position. I curl up on the ground. My muscles scream in agony when I move them, so I stay as still as possible.

"Sarka." The voice comes from a speaker above us. It takes me a minute before I realize where I've heard that name before.

"Yes?" He turns from me, and I can no longer see his face, just the back of his head. A large jagged scar runs from the edge of his hairline down below his collar. I had heard a lot of the Burrs, when they first came back from war, tried to remove some of their implants. I wonder if he was trying to remove his own mind knot. When he's finished speaking into the intercom, he turns back to me, and I'm facing the hard blue eyes of Davis Sarka, leader of the Burrs. I've read everything there is in the database about him—which is extensive before and during the wars, but brief and almost nonexistent after.

He was born on Earth in a place called Bar Harbor, Maine, and I immediately envy him that. He's seen Earth from the ground, felt the sun on his face. He's experienced rain, thunderstorms, lightning, and ocean waves. Things I've only read about, but know are nothing unless experienced firsthand.

Sarka has spent most of his life in one army or another. When he was sixteen, he used a fake ID to enlist in the Air Force. But it wasn't until he turned eighteen that they realized he hadn't graduated from high school. By that time, it didn't matter. Earth's final wars had started, and the military needed everybody they could get their hands on.

When he was twenty-one, he led an assault over what was left of the Great Lakes. His plane was shot down, and he had to ditch into the dirt field of what was once Lake Ontario. He was captured and tortured for one hundred and eighty-eight days.

I don't want to find out how bad this is going to get. He must have an entire torture playbook filed in the recesses of his memory.

"Take your clothes off."

As soon as he says it, my skin goes clammy. As I stand here, I can feel the hardness of the wall at my back, I can even feel the smooth rivets digging into my hand, but I have no control over what I'll do. I am only a spectator.

"I've filled a bucket with water in my washroom. You can wash." He points to his bed. There's a fresh uniform folded on the corner. "I took the liberty of getting one from your cabin. I hope you don't mind."

I still haven't moved from the wall.

"It reminded me of my daughter's room. She always liked collecting trinkets from Earth."

I'm both surprised and fascinated by this revelation. Surprised that he has a daughter—I thought all Burrs were sterile—and fascinated because it's such a personal admission.

"I'm not going to undress you, but you will wash, even if I have to pour the water over your head." He grabs my arm and drags me into the washroom. It's smaller than I expected. There's only a sink and a tap near the floor, with a drain under it. Next to the tap is a five-liter bucket filled to the brim, and a sponge and bar of soap next to it on the floor. "The stuff in the green bottle is for your hair." He releases my bindings and leans against the door, blocking it.

He's not going to undress me, but he is going to watch. I dip my fingers in the water. It's lukewarm. Better than cold, I guess. Without looking at him I say, "Is this a trade? I give you the passcode, and you let me wash in privacy?"

The skin on his face stretches in what must be his version of a smile. "Now you're getting it."

CHAPTER SIXTEEN

When I'm naked, I grab the sponge and plunge it into the bucket. I slather it with the soap. It smells like pears. My skin pinks and reddens under the assault of scrubbing. My toes curl around the edges of the drain. There's a shallow circle of clean grout around the splash radius of the tap, but everywhere else the grout is a grungy charcoal black.

By the time I get to my hair, I've got goose bumps on my arms and legs. The room is colder. "I'm not going to wash my hair."

"I'd like you to wash your hair, Alison."

A tremor ripples down my spine, and I wrap my arms across my breasts. I shake my head.

Quick before I can block him, he lunges for me. Gripping the back of my neck, he shoves me to the ground. My head barely misses the sink protruding out of the wall. I struggle against him, grabbing for his arm, but my feet slip and my knees crash into the hard cold tile, sending a shock wave through my bones. I reach for his wrists, digging my nails into his skin. He slams my cheek into the tile. I scramble to get out from under him, groping and slapping at anything I can reach.

He catches my flailing arms, pins them, and sits on my back, crushing me to the floor. With his free hand, he squirts pear-scented shampoo over my greasy hair and rubs it into the cold, wet tile. He pours water over my head and continues to knead until flecks of foam spray my cheek. I push up with my hips, trying to dislodge him, but he's too heavy, and I sink back to the floor. I grind my teeth, seething. The cold seeps into my skin from the tile. He pours more water over my head to rinse the shampoo away. It runs icy trails down my back. I buck again and pull one arm free. I reach out and tip the bucket away from me. It spills into the drain. He hauls me up by my neck and arm, and slams me against the wall, pinning me flat with his body between the sink and the tap. He twists the tap. Frigid water splashes over my feet. The bulk of him makes the tiny room appear even smaller.

I want to give in. How easy it would be to surrender the passcode and give up the schematics to the plasma pulse. One slip. Only one slip from me, and we would lose the war against the Burrs. Our new technology is our only real defense. To give in now would be to give up and change the future for everyone.

His hand clamps my chin, squeezing it between his thumb and fingers. "This can all end, Alison, you can make that choice." His breath hits my ear. The stench is a mixture of pear and whatever else he's eaten that day. I yank my face away. My hair and body stink of pear. It overpowers my senses, and I gag.

"You make it stop, Alison! You make it stop, Alison!" Each time it gets louder until he's shouting into my ear.

It's hearing my name that does it. I scream and then scream again until I have no voice left, until my throat is raw, until I'm exhausted and all I want to do is bawl in frustration and humiliation. I scream until I have no energy left to give up the passcode.

Later, while half my brain is thinking of pudding, the other is acutely aware of Sarka's movements in the other room. I can hear the knock on his door and the man who enters, and I'm starting to anticipate what happens next because it's not new. This has all happened before.

They stop in the doorway. I keep my eyes shut and my breathing even.

"Is she dead?" The second voice is higher than Sarka's; he sounds younger. I resist the urge to look.

"No."

"We need her alive for this to work." He sounds agitated.

"I'm aware." Sarka leaves the doorway, and the other man follows. When they resume their conversation, their voices are muffled.

I crawl to the other side of the room to eavesdrop. Air hits my hidden bits as soon as I move, and my teeth begin to chatter. I clasp a hand over my mouth and kneel beside the door to catch the last bit of what they're saying.

"The transmitter's working. Although we won't know if the rest of it's working until she's aboard the *Persephone*."

Sarka grunts.

"At least it's transmitting, so if it doesn't work, we'll know right away." Transmitter? They must be talking about the mind knot, which means it's already been implanted inside me. And then it hits me what they're actually saying. The mind knot's transmitting data back to them. If it's connected to my brainstem, does that mean they have access to everything in my brain? I'll have to ask Dr. Prashad how all that works.

"And the vial? How will she get access to that?"

"It'll be in the lining of her duffel."

"And she'll detonate it?"

Detonate? Was that what I was supposed to do to Hartley? Or is it still something I'm meant to do?

"If she's close enough."

I quietly crawl back before Sarka catches me listening. And of course, I knew all this before I boarded the *Persephone*, but they programmed the mind knot to release chemicals that inhibited these memories. The day I stepped over the threshold, I was as ignorant as the rest of the crew.

What would they have done if I hadn't gotten medical clearance from Alpha to be released? I lay my head back on my knees and tuck my arms between them to gain some warmth. I guess it would've been another job for the mind knot.

Sometime later Sarka squats in front of me. My uniform is tucked under one arm. One of his hands is missing the tip of his pinky and ring finger. Is that something that happened during battle, or something they did to him when he was captured and tortured? How did he survive a hundred and eighty-eight days? I'm barely holding on now, and I know I haven't remembered everything. Bits and pieces are missing from my mind, too horrible to relive, and I'm thankful I still have a little self-preservation left.

He reaches out, and I flinch, but he doesn't hit me. Instead, he runs the back of his fingers across my cheek. My chest tightens and my chin trembles. For a second, I feel…comforted. I don't want to cry, but sob anyway. The anger and hate I can cope with, but not this, not this sick perversion of kindness.

And then he removes his hand. There's a soft thump to my right. He's thrown my uniform on the floor.

"Get dressed." He retreats to the door to watch, but it's with a disinterested eye, like someone watching a ship dock.

"It doesn't matter what you do." I slip on my uniform pants; the warmth coats my skin like a protective shield. "I won't tell you how to access the station's computer."

He spins me and grabs my wrists together behind my back to bind them with something hard and plastic. It digs into my skin.

I'm silent as he escorts me down the corridors. We pass through several small workstations. There aren't any women at the stations. I know there are women Burrs, but not many.

He stops in front of a door, and when they open, we're back in the room with the rod. I dig my feet into the cold metal floor, trying to resist, but he pushes me inside.

"Your wife, was she a Burr, too?"

"My wife?" He unbinds me and shoves me into the chair.

"The woman...who gave birth to your daughter."

"No, she wasn't." I can't imagine anyone willingly giving themselves to this man. Was she held against her will?

Reading my thoughts, he says, "No, Alison, I didn't rape her."

He enters a sequence of numbers into the panel, and the chair tilts back again. When I'm lying flat, he inserts a large syringe into my arm and tells me it's a paralyzing agent. I'll be able to breathe, but all my muscles except my heart have been paralyzed. I feel it taking effect after a few seconds. I try to move my arm, but only manage to shift it to the right a bit.

He places a mask that creates an airtight seal around my mouth and nose. It's attached to a small canister that sits on my chest. With each breath I take, I receive less and less air. After three, I feel a familiar panic as I try to pull air into my lungs. There's a painful clamp on my chest, like an explosion building from inside my lungs.

My eyes fill with tears, but I can't blink them away. My vision blurs. He becomes a shape, a blob of color standing beside me until the liquid spills over and drools down my cheeks. Just when I think I'm about to pass out, Sarka reaches out and releases the air seal. I drink in air like it's water.

"Twelve characters, Alison, that's all I need to hear from you, and this will end. You can have a proper shower, a full meal, and a clean bed."

Even if I wanted to, I couldn't speak. He must realize that's what I'm thinking because he holds up another syringe. "This will reverse the paralyzing agent. All you have to do is grunt, Alison, and I will use this"—he indicates the syringe—"instead of this," and he holds up the mask.

I don't make a sound.

He places the mask over my face again, as there's a knock at the door. I'm only vaguely aware of the man that enters. From his voice, I know it's the one from earlier.

"It worked," he says. He's excited about something.

I pull the last of the air from the canister, focusing on what they're saying, but it's becoming difficult.

"We hacked her passcode," he says.

CHAPTER SEVENTEEN

I enter the bridge, overwhelmed as if it's the first time. The view from the panoramic windows is breathtaking. It's almost like there are more stars than space. They pepper the expanse like a jeweler's cloth sprinkled with diamonds. I imagine each of them as a sun, each with the possibility of planets and life. The idea is intoxicating.

I make a quick scan and confirm the captain isn't here before taking a seat at one of the stations. Dr. Prashad said she wanted me to check in before duty, which can't be a good thing. I have a bad feeling the next words out of her mouth are going to include the phrase "relieved of duty," and I have far too much to do to let that happen.

Before coming to the bridge, I stopped by my cabin. The vial the Burrs placed in my duffel bag back on Europa station is no longer there—only a rip—which means there's a good possibility I've already used it. I need to check the video footage of when I attacked Hartley. I know there wasn't any from the actual assault, but Hartley said I wasn't captured until I got to the airlock. That's a lot of space to cover, and there's sure to be footage between the attack and the airlock.

I spend the next hour sorting through that day's security camera recordings until finally, I catch the images. It's quick, and I have to replay it a few times before I can understand what I'm seeing. I pause it mid-action and see myself tossing a syringe behind a stand of canisters next to the airlock.

"Lieutenant Ash."

I jump and scramble to shut off my screen, then turn to see Jordan standing at the entrance to the bridge.

"Can I speak with you in private?"

Shit. I stand to follow her off the bridge. She looks pissed.

Before I get to the door, Vasa calls out to her that there's something she should see.

"I'll only be a minute, you can tell me when I'm back," she answers.

He swivels back to check his monitor, undecided if he should push further, but whatever is on his screen makes him brave. "Okay. It's just, is this the anomaly you wanted me to watch out for? There's a trace of it behind us."

She steps around me toward Vasa. I think she's forgotten that I'm there until she calls out for me to wait in her cabin. But as soon as the doors shut and I'm free from sight, I sprint along the corridor to the first deck chute. I scramble down so fast I miss the third rung and almost slip off. I hold tight, regain my footing, and continue in a much more controlled descent.

The airlock is deserted when I arrive. I crouch behind the crate of air canisters on hands and knees in search of the syringe that I now know, due to the footage, I chucked after attacking Hartley. I sweep my hand under the canisters back and forth, each wide arc moving deeper until my shoulder stops me from going farther, and my fingers catch the tip of something hard. I wrap my hand around it and pull it out. It looks like every other syringe I've seen. The vial, however, is blank on its label, with only a hint of liquid slipping down the insides as I turn it about.

As I watch, mesmerized by the sway of the pale blue froth, it hits me, what happened, what I did to Hartley the day I attacked him in the corridor. I need to know what's in this vial.

I rush back to the med center, aware that I'm trackable, aware, too, that whoever they send for me will be less understanding now that I've disobeyed a direct order. Around each turn, each bend, I expect to meet Vasa lined by two security guards and the barrel of their guns pointed at me. But I don't; my route is deserted.

When I arrive, the doctor is seated by a monitor scrolling through data. If I'm not mistaken, it's my own readings from my first dose. I recognize the mountain peak next to the hills. The doctor is comparing these to new peaks and valleys, and I assume it's my latest trip under that he's collating.

"Dr. Prashad." I'm out of breath and I don't know why. It must be the adrenaline, the thrill of getting caught that makes my heart beat and my palms sweat. "I need you to analyze the contents of this," I say, placing the vial on the table in front of him.

He takes it, turning it in the light, curious now. "Where did you find it?"

"It came on board with me."

The doctor sets it on the table and opens a drawer, rummaging through its contents until he pulls out an instrument to open the top of the vial. "And you don't know what's in it? Even though you brought it with you?"

I hop on one of the beds to watch him work, keeping an eye on the doors the whole time. Maybe if they track me now, they'll think I got sick and came here. Maybe I won't get Vasa's armed guards. "It was hidden in my duffel lining," I say. "I think I stabbed Hartley to cover the injection site, just like the Burrs used my wound to hide the mind knot entry point."

Dr. Prashad swabs the inside of the glass and slips it into a long black cylinder. "So whatever's in here could be in Hartley right now?"

I shrug, because based on what I overheard none of this makes sense. They said if I was close enough I would detonate it. Where's the bomb I'm meant to detonate? Is it on board the *Posterus* already? Are they going to take me over as soon as we get there? And if I did inject Hartley with whatever's in this syringe, how is that supposed to help? The screen on the cylinder in his hand lights up, green against black, with a medley of numbers and letters, running through the molecules hidden in the soft folds of the swab.

"I examined Hartley after the attack, I didn't see anything unusual—aside from the stab wound in his lower back, of course."

I cringe and look down at my fingers. I have to keep reminding myself that it wasn't me who did that. "Was he in a lot of pain?"

"Yes," Dr. Prashad says. But as soon as he sees the horror on my face, he softens. "It was only momentary. The cut was so superficial it's almost like it never happened."

But it did, and I was the one to do it.

As soon as the cylinder cycles through its task, the doctor taps it against the monitor, transferring the information to the screen. A new display comes up, most of which I can't understand. He's busy for a second, scrolling through, hands flying, muttering to himself. I leave him to it, wishing that he'd hurry. He pulls up a new file and swipes through several screens of this with a few more grunts and a couple of *reallys* and *imagines*. I can't take any more suspense, I slide off the bed.

"What is it?" I ask.

"It looks like…" He shakes his head like he must be wrong, and flips through a few more screens before stopping at a list of chemicals, some of which I do recognize. At the top of that list, and the most disconcerting, is nitrosamine.

"What is that a list of?"

"It's what was in the vial, but it's also," and he pulls up another screen, "now laced throughout Hartley's body. This here," he points to a word I don't recognize, "is a synthetic binder. It's binding the nitrosamine to Hartley's tendons and bones as if the substance has fused with his system."

"Wouldn't you have recognized a carcinogen in his system when you examined him the first time?"

"Not in such trace amounts. You'd be surprised at the things your body collects without you knowing it. But the problem here is that it's spreading through him like a virus. I think the vial contained some sort of nanotechnology to replicate this stuff and infuse his body."

And just like that, I know what I'm meant to detonate. My stomach muscles clench as my mind flies in a million directions, grabbing hold of elusive what-ifs.

I'm meant to detonate Hartley.

"And more worrying still is what I found laced through your system."

"What?"

He shakes his head as if he's not sure, or more likely doesn't want to be. "We all create a small amount of electricity in our bodies. Not enough, mind you, to be of much use, but what I'm seeing in yours is that you've got an abnormal build-up of protons—positively charged particles. That's abnormal in itself because usually your body…"

He's searching for a way to describe this so I'm not completely lost. But it's too late for that.

"Just tell me what you think it means."

"It means that if this keeps up, and you happen to touch Hartley, your body combined with his will act as an explosive."

Chapter Eighteen

My fingers tremble as I punch in my activation code for the escape pod. An inappropriately perky chime fills the cramped space as the welcome screen fades.

I'm the other half of a bomb.

I have to get away from Hartley before we blow up the ship. The thought rolls around my head like a billiard ball off the break, knocking and bumping until my mind is a racket of clicking and clangs. How did this all go so wrong? When I stepped aboard the *Persephone*, I would never have imagined that I would be sitting here, only a few weeks later, in an escape pod, about to commit suicide. I take a deep, shaky breath at that thought.

That is what I'm going to do. I've decided to launch a pod that will hurtle through space with no propulsion, no sensors, no navigation. And no way to detect space debris, let alone avoid it, which probably is the whole point. The surprise of death is better than knowing when and how you'll die. There is food enough for two weeks, but only air enough for seventy-two hours. Whoever designed these escape pods clearly had a sense of humor. I will die of oxygen deprivation long before I die of starvation—if I don't explode from a collision first. These pods were meant to be lifebuoys. They have one function, and that is to keep you alive until a rescue ship arrives. But there is no rescue ship coming for me.

After several warning screens, the countdown flashes green, waiting for me to hit the go button. Once it's pressed, I'll have three minutes before the door closes and the pod unlatches from the ship. I hesitate over the panel. *Is this reckless?* Am I being too rash to think that there won't be a better solution?

I can't think of any other way to save the ship. Prashad said there was no way to unbind the nitrosamine from Hartley's system or stop the micro-parasites slinking through my system and persuading my subatomic particles to create a potential motherlode of electric shocks. There is only one way. Only one way I can stop the Burrs—stop Sarka from using me to destroy the ship we have worked so hard to protect the past two decades.

I press the panel and start the sequence.

I strap myself into the control chair—which is laughable—there's nothing to control once this thing gets going. The buckles close with a final-sounding click. The metal is cold against my shaking hands, and I breathe to push the dread, clogged in my throat, back down.

"What the hell are you doing?"

I turn to see Jordan standing in the door, with panic in her eyes. They're wide, the pupils tiny pinpricks lost in an expanse of blue. Her chest is heaving. She's out of breath from running and her raven black hair now looks like a dark nebula, an interstellar cloud of dust—it has no clear boundaries and reaches in all directions.

I try to concentrate. Escape pods are most definitely off-limits. She must have rushed from the bridge. I wonder if Vasa is close behind.

I reach down feeling for the mass in my cargo pocket. When my fingers wrap around the cool cylinder, a calm descends. "Have you spoken with Dr. Prashad?"

"He messaged me on the bridge." She pivots the control chair so we're face-to-face, and that's when she notices the countdown on the screen behind me. Her mouth drops open, dumbfounded. She looks to me as if she can't believe I'd do something so brainless. She catches a glimpse of the restraints anchoring me to the pod. "Are you insane?" Her voice is a low hiss. There's a pause where we stare, inches apart, and then a flurry of action as she unfastens the harness and yanks me from the chair. I'm so stunned that it takes me a moment before I resist her touch.

"This is the only way," I say, jerking my arm free from her grasp. I hold the back of the chair, just in case she tries to pull me out of the pod.

"I doubt that. There's nothing that would convince me to help you…"

Kill yourself. She can't say it, but I know that's what she means. I am shaking with fear but determination, too. I have to save the ship. But part of me—a large part—wishes I could take her in the pod with me, that we could be safe together. Somewhere. "Only this way I can at least save the lives of hundreds, maybe thousands of people."

She shakes her head, confused, the idea that my death could save thousands unfathomable. I wish I had more time. I need her to understand that this is for the best, but I'm not a saint, every second I delay the easier it is for her to talk me out of it. Just her presence has me second-guessing myself.

"There's no way I'm leaving this pod, not alive anyway," I say.

She steps back as if I've punched her, and there's more than fear and panic in her eyes now. I've seen that look directed at me enough times to know she's furious.

"We'll keep you apart. We'll make sure you and Hartley are never in the same room. I promise you I will make sure of this."

I shake my head. I've thought of all this. "And what if my

mind knot takes over and I don't have a choice? We can't take that risk. Or are you planning on locking me up in the brig for the rest of my life?"

"Once we're out of range of the communication buoys we'll..." And then her mind catches on to what I've already discovered: The *Posterus* will be dropping communication buoys along our flight path in an attempt to remain in contact with the Union fleet.

It's such an unsettling contrast to see her spirited presence—with the ebony hair and shining blue uniform—against a backdrop of sterile walls and panels. And all the while, her mind must be charging as quickly as a bursting gamma ray.

"You can't do this." She's desperate to find a solution that doesn't involve me shooting into the unknown in a glorified casket.

My mouth dries. "It's done." I must save the ship. It's the only way to plug the gaping hole, the aching hole that's torn me up since I found out what happened to me on Sarka's ship. And then I remember once more the reason I won't fight anymore. I am no longer whole.

I remind myself: *I am the other half of a bomb.*

This fact has ripped me up, and no matter what, I will never be able to become whole again.

Jordan's head falls to her chest. She's beautiful in this moment, and I take it as a last gift. One last time to be near her. The pale high cheekbones, colored by emotion, the long dark lashes stark against her skin.

"We just need more time," she says.

I look back at the countdown again, only a minute left. "This is all we have."

"You horrify me, Ash. The things you're willing to do to yourself."

I try to protest, but she raises her hand for me to stop.

"From the first time I met you. You always push yourself to

extremes!" She doesn't move toward me, just hugs her arms tight against her chest. "Well, I don't accept this. There's a solution that doesn't require you to die."

"You don't have a choice!"

"I'm ordering you to get off this pod and to report to the doctor. Right now!" She grabs my wrist. "You're relieved of duty."

I watch her rush through emotions as if she's shuffling a deck of cards, and a strange numbness settles over me. I am an empty container; nothing left to fill me except the void of space. I almost laugh.

"Or what?" I ask. "What are you going to do? Court-martial me?"

I check the countdown, only forty-five seconds left. "Leave, Jordan."

Jordan somehow manages to reach past me and enter her command code on the computer. She's the only person on this ship who can stop the countdown of an escape pod. Too late, I push her away. But it's done. The count stops at thirty-three seconds.

"Why did you do that?" I yell. "If that engine blows up, this mission will be set back years, maybe forever. The mission is worth my sacrifice."

"But why does it have to be you? Why are you always so quick to sacrifice yourself?"

"I don't know! I don't know, okay?" I sink down into the pilot's seat. All the exhaustion and stress from the last couple of weeks deflates. "I was raised that way, I guess. In my family, if there's something that needs to be done, we do it, because we can."

"That's a harsh way to live, Ash."

I close my eyes. I can't look at her. "Every single person in my family has served, going back as far as we can remember. Me in the fleet, my father in the Commons, my grandfather led the first wave of immigrants to the Belt back in the early twenties. I joined the fleet because I knew it was what was required of me."

"Is that why you're doing this? For approval?" She's incredulous; she doesn't understand.

Is that why I'm doing this? For some deep-seated need to prove that I'm worthy to my family? No, it's more than that.

"Because if it is, I can tell you right now, it's not worth it," Jordan says. "The price is too high."

I open my eyes. "It sounds like a price *you've* had to pay."

She leans against the console, folding her arms. "I've never understood the need to seek approval from one's family." She sucks her bottom lip into her mouth, contemplating. "Then again, my father was never worthy of it."

"Why not? What did he do?" This feels absurd. Only a moment ago I was ready to sacrifice my life, and yet here I am with someone…someone I'm falling in love with. I want to know her. I want to be close to her before I die. I want this. And I will convince her I must go.

Her face drains of color as she looks out the porthole. "It's more like, what didn't he do?" She runs her hands along the console as if she's looking for dust to wipe clean. "I was ten when I first noticed something was wrong. My dad had these charts of the solar system, made of real paper. And he was always poring over them, which naturally made me fascinated by them as well. One day I was looking at them when no one was around. They didn't make any sense to me, but they were beautiful. Whoever created them had used a different color to map out different phenomenon, where radiation was the worst, where a planet's gravity well started. Reaching out to grab another one, I accidentally spilled my juice over them. I tried to wipe it up, but that only made it worse.

"When my mom found me, she was livid. I'd never seen her so mad. But it wasn't so much that she was angry at me. She was scared for me...and herself. I'd never noticed it before then, and I don't know why I never picked up on it. My mom was terrified of my father. She never looked directly at him, always stared at the ground in front of his feet, the wall beside his head, or me. She barely spoke to him, only when he asked her a direct question. When he was away on scout missions, she'd rest easier, not like other wives who might be afraid their husbands might never come back. She was more afraid that he would. And I realized then that it wasn't just my mom who was scared of him, I was, too. It wasn't until much later, when I lived on Delta, that I discovered it's not natural for kids to be afraid of their parents."

"Did he find out about the juice?"

"If he did, I never heard about it. I have no idea if my mother was able to fix it or she took the blame herself. Either way, he never did anything about it."

"Would he have?"

She shakes her head. More locks come loose, framing her perfectly pale face. "It doesn't matter now. It was a long time ago. Talking about it doesn't change anything."

I reach out and place my hand over hers. It stops her sweeping motion. "It might help, to open up about it." Her hand is warm under mine and so soft.

"I don't need to talk about it, Ash. I gave up that family when I joined Union fleet."

I stand, wrapping my hand around her wrist. The skin on the inside of her wrist is the softest I've ever felt.

There's a brief pause, almost as if she's adjusting to the new sensation before she says, "This is my family now. It's the only one that matters."

I run my hand lightly up her forearm. "Then you see why I need to do this. This is my family now, too. When I signed onto this mission, I left my old family behind. And the only way to keep this family safe is to leave."

I take a step toward her, closing the gap, and tilt my head up. My lips brush against hers so softly that it's a ghost of a kiss. We stare, inches apart, as the time we have left together gets shorter.

Her lips crash against mine. Her hand wraps around the back of my neck and holds me near. Heat rips through me, turning on every light, igniting every fire. I don't dare move. The feeling of her, soft and pliant against me, is unexpected. I push her up on the console. Her legs part and I move between them, closing as much space between us as I can. I wish it was her skin I was feeling, and not the rough, unforgiving fabric of our uniforms. I wish we weren't in an escape pod and this wasn't a stolen moment, that we had all the time in the world to explore what we've started.

I kiss her lips with more force now, as if it were our last. And the thought drifts to the surface—it is our last. The last time I will see her, feel her. I will never again hear her laugh, smell her scent of apricots. Never again see those blue eyes narrowed in anger or laughter, never feel her soft, warm lips against mine. Her legs wrap around me, and I want to forget where we are.

I give our kiss everything I have left.

Her lips part and my breath catches. The heat building fills the hole inside me momentarily—until I'm pulled back to reality.

I need to leave.

Before it goes too far, before I make my wish to feel her skin against mine a reality, I reach into my pocket and pull out the syringe I stole from the med center. I break our kiss and tilt her head, and bend to plant a single kiss along her neck. Her eyes are closed, her dark lashes flutter against her cheeks, her lips, red and swollen, part, and before she opens her eyes, I push the point of the syringe into her neck and plunge the milky liquid into her system.

There's a moment before she collapses into my arms, and the look of betrayal cuts me in half. I drag her out into the corridor and rest her on the ground. I step back into the pod, and the doors close between us.

I restart the countdown sequence. I strap myself in for the last time, the click the last thing I hear before the blasting whoosh as the pod's ejection pack erupts and sends us, me and the pod, hurtling toward the unknown.

CHAPTER NINETEEN

My hand flies to the back of my neck, my fingers scraping against clammy skin. The mind knot. It must have transmitted my position, and I've only been flying in the pod less than six hours. I turn in horror toward the hatch. Four thunderous clangs come from the other side, one after the other. They've attached four magnets to hold the pod in place while they create an airtight seal and cut the door open. I have to figure out how to stop Sarka from getting me, but I have some time. How much, I don't know.

From the porthole, I can see the Burrs' flagship. Its elongated bow stretches before me, the matter sails patched and frayed. Half the ship has been rebuilt from scraps stolen from Union ships. I can even make out parts of Europa station welded to the hull. They're shinier than the rest of the ship, reflecting the expanse of stars surrounding us.

This far out, there isn't much light from the sun. It's like being enclosed in one of the crystal caves on Alpha, cocooned in darkness with millions of bright twinkles catching your eye everywhere you look.

If I'd known this was how it would end, knowing Sarka would be on my trail, would I have chosen differently? Would I have listened to Jordan? Probably not. Though I want to imagine staying, wrapped in that kiss. I ignore the vast emptiness stretching before me, close my thoughts to the menacing screeches coming behind me and imagine—for just a moment—what it would be like if I weren't me. If I weren't the stubborn lieutenant my father raised. If instead of years worrying how to make everyone else happy, I had just gone my own way, would I still be here now? In this predicament? Or would I have found a nice, quiet place to settle down and live my life?

That idea sounds more unappealing than where I am now.

I release my harness. My body floats in the new lack of gravity. I forgot the pods don't have artificial gravity. I launch from the control chair and swim as best I can toward the panels behind the passenger seats. I need to find something to blast the window out. Even the tiniest hole will decompress the cabin and suck everything—including me—out a window the size of a cantaloupe. If that doesn't kill me, any number of things will.

If I don't empty my lungs of air before I'm sucked out, they'll expand rapidly in the low-pressure environment, popping like a balloon. Because there's no humidity in space, every exposed liquid will freeze instantly: my sweat will crystallize, my eyes will freeze, my respiratory tract will ice over. I don't even want to think of what will happen below the waist. But that's nothing compared to the liquid that's hidden away inside my body. It will expand, forming water vapor, bloating me to twice my size. And since the boiling point lowers the less pressure there is in the atmosphere, in space, it's entirely possible the temperature of my body will be enough to boil my blood.

I catch the ledge of the ceiling and hold on while I open one of the storage compartments. Loose items drift out and bob along like ice floating to the surface in a glass of lemonade. I'm not sure what I'm looking for. We don't keep any weapons on board, and even if we did, they wouldn't be strong enough to crack metallic glass. I just know I'll recognize it when I see it. What most people don't know is that these escape pods are very much like the original lunar modules used in the first missions to the moon. They're lightweight and utterly flimsy. It doesn't take much to breach them. And that's when I find it. My hand tightens around a manual jack, and I tug it out of the compartment. In an emergency situation, it's used to jack the hatch open if the pod loses power, but I think I've found a better use for it.

I glide back toward the window, open the winch on the jack, and wind it until it fits snugly between the window frames. If I can wedge the frame apart—a more likely scenario than blowing a hole in glass ten inches thick—I might fracture the structure enough to decompress the cabin.

A deafening screech fills my ears as I turn and see they've started cutting into the hatch. If I time this right, I might be able to take out more than myself.

Jordan's words surface for an instant. It scares me too, the things I'm willing to do to myself. But I usually don't let myself think of the consequences. I just seize the fence and hold tight. She wouldn't have put herself in this position in the first place. She would've thought everything through before stepping foot on this escape pod.

With a determination that has me out of breath, I swing the winch, fast. The grinding and creaking of the window's frame commingle with the screeching behind me. It's now a race. Will they breach the hatch before I decompress the cabin? As I watch the handle turn, and the gap between both edges of the jack widen, I'm reminded of something Sarka said that first time, about humans not appreciating the simple things in life. And this is so simple. I'm using probably one of the earliest pieces of technology humans ever invented, to create a fissure that will suck me out into space, ending all thoughts, all pain. Just ending it all. And this should be a calming thought. But it's not, because for whatever reason, our big brains, our abstract thought, our imagination, whatever it is that makes humans different, makes us strive for more, also makes us complicate the hell out of everything.

I'm sweating now. Droplets run down my temple and cheek, pooling at my jaw. I'm almost crying from the effort and stress of it all. Just a little more to go. I'm not thinking about the results anymore. I have a goal. Everything slows. Three more turns. The hatch behind me falls forward with a clank. Two more turns. I hear angry shouting behind me. One more turn. A pain so profound, so all consuming hits and spreads from my lower back. I collapse to my knees, as the gravity from the ship takes hold. Still holding tight to the winch, I try for one last swing. Something slams into the back of my head…and then nothing.

❖

My hands are shackled behind my back and connected to a chain on the wall above me. I should be used to waking up in cells by now, except nothing can prepare you for the fear of not knowing what will be on the other side of that door when it opens.

When it does open, Four-Teeth is on the other side. I recognize him more from his stench than his lack of teeth. He squats in front of me, and I have a good view of his boots. There's a splash of red on the worn tip that I hope isn't blood.

"Oh, you noticed that, did you?" he asks, grabbing my hair and pulling my head off the floor, forcing me to look up at him.

I can't help it, I groan. I feel as if I've been thrashed with a mallet.

"It's yours, just so's you know. A happy little souvenir of our time together." He pushes me on my back, his eyes traveling over my torso, pausing briefly at my breasts before inching down farther, and that's when I notice I'm only wearing an undershirt and briefs. One thought races through my mind, and my heart thumps so loud I can hear it shaking between my ears. If he reaches for me, I've got enough leverage to flip my hips up and wrap my legs around his neck. If I'm fast enough, maybe I'll break his neck before he knows what's happened.

"Down, boy," comes a deep, gravelly voice from behind. "You're about two seconds away from a lot of pain."

I'm surprised when the source of the voice turns out to be a woman. She looks older than the rest of the Burrs, with long, scraggly hair, white except for the odd streak of black. Her almond eyes are almost lost in the folds of her wrinkled olive skin. The wrinkles alone set her apart.

Four-Teeth grins. "And who's the one doling out the pain, you old woman?"

The woman points a leathery finger at me. "Never turn your back on a trapped tiger." She steps closer and kicks him lightly, inclining her head toward the door.

"Whatever." He stands but pauses, looking down at me, not sure if he really wants to go. A sly grin spreads his mouth.

I shudder. My skin becomes cold in the dark room. I wait until he's gone before I ask, "How did you know?"

"I can monitor parts of your brain." She points to a small tablet tucked under her arm. When she kneels down beside me, her gaze roams over my body, much as Four-Teeth's did, only hers is assessing. There's nothing predatory about it. She places the container from under her other arm on the ground and begins sorting its contents like she's lining up chess pieces.

"From the mind knot?"

She nods.

"How much can you see?"

She shrugs, still setting out objects. "It depends."

"Depends on what?"

She turns me on my stomach, brushing my hair off the back of my neck with gentle fingers.

"The mind knot transmits your brain scans. How much I see is dependent on how much I can interpret." Her voice is close to my ear as she leans in. I flinch as she brushes something along the wound on the back of my skull. "For instance, just now, your amygdala lit up, which among other things is a center for aggression. And also your putamen, which is where learned skills are stored. I can interpret that as preparation for an attack." She stops swabbing and pours a liquid over the wound on my head. I grit my teeth at the sting. "Each emotion you experience lights up different areas of your brain, and I can monitor that."

"You've been monitoring my emotions?"

"Among other things."

"What other things?"

She tut-tuts me instead of answering. For the next several minutes she works in silence, first bandaging my head and then moving down to my lower back. I'd forgotten about the searing pain. I must have been hit with some sort of weapon. It feels like the sting of a burn.

Finally, I get up the courage to ask what I really want. "Were you born on Earth?"

"Yes, in a little town in Japan...Kushima." She says the name as if she's rolling a sweet around her mouth as if it's the last time she'll taste it on her tongue. It breaks my heart.

"What was it like?"

She tuts me again. But instead of ignoring the question, she begins speaking. Like the tide coming in, it's slow at first. "We lived on what used to be the coast of Shibushi Bay. I remember as a child walking to where our boat was anchored, several kilometers out, where the Pacific met dry ocean beds. There wasn't much to fish, but we were better off than most." Her gnarled fingers play with the top button of her tunic. "It was my job to measure the distance to the boat. I kept hoping the water would come closer, so we wouldn't have to walk so far. But every year the trek would get longer—the shoreline, farther away."

"What was the ocean like?"

"Dirty. What wasn't polluted by chemicals was coated with

flotsam. Some of it was useful, but most of it was just trash… Sometimes, though…" Her voice softens, as does her expression. "Sometimes, after a particularly strong hurricane, the skies would clear to a dark azure, and the water would sparkle, like sequins on a dress, shimmying through the waves."

"It must have been beautiful."

The lines around her mouth crease deeper. She doesn't answer this time. Instead she turns away to finish packing her supplies.

Chapter Twenty

Four-Teeth grabs me and twists, slamming me against the wall. He locks my wrists in a tight grip. "You are one dumb bitch. How did you make first officer anyway?" He pushes his face close to mine as he growls. "Those are your screams. Or don't you remember the last time you were here?"

I struggle to get my wrists free, but he digs his shoulder into my neck. We stall in this position. His breath creeps down my cheek as he pants in my ear. I can feel his eyes on me, but I keep mine shut tight.

As far as escapes go, this hasn't gone according to plan. If I had to pinpoint the beginning of this downward spiral, it would be the screaming. I'd just raided their laundry for an oversized uniform when I heard what I thought was screaming coming from one of the other holding cells. They'd set a trap, knowing I'd investigate.

"You don't deserve to wear this uniform. It's for heroes only, you coward." Four-Teeth snarls into the back of my head.

"How am I a coward?"

"You ran. You ran from the greatest honor, to become a martyr and hero. We don't belong out there. Humans belong on Earth. We belong to this sun and this solar system."

I snort at that. What a load of propaganda bullshit. "If it's a hero's uniform, why are you wearing one?" He doesn't like that.

He grinds into me, holding me tight against the wall while his hands snake down to the button of my pants. I spin as much as I can, clawing at his wrists, tugging them off me. There's a flurry of pulling and scraping. I hear the tearing of fabric, and to my mortification, a great big sob escapes, and I'm gasping for air. It only makes him laugh and struggle harder to get my pants off.

"Everette!" Sarka's voice booms through the speakers above us. Four-Teeth freezes. "Haven't you found her yet?"

I can see the debate in his eyes, wondering if he has enough time. Luckily for me he decides not, and I collapse on the floor gulping for air, tears streaming down my face.

"Take him to medical." He points to the crumpled man on the ground, before pulling me to my feet and marching me forward.

I glare in hatred at the faces in front of me, Four-Teeth, whose real name, Everette, doesn't seem to match the big oaf, and Sarka, his face and expression tighter than ever. We're in Sarka's office. Behind him is a large window, and the view is spectacular. The sun is very far off, only a small yellow globe now. This far out, there's only emptiness and isolation. We truly are alone. Very few fleet ships ever venture this far. It would take too long to get help if needed.

I catch my reflection in the glass and notice the beginnings of a black eye. Awesome.

"I underestimated you." Sarka pauses studying me. His hand glides along the stubble on his jaw. "Or maybe I overestimated Everette."

Everette shifts, keeping his hand on his gun hilt. His eyes stare with equal hatred into mine.

There's a lot of quiet contemplation and staring going on before Sarka finally speaks again. "This must all be a little confusing for you."

I cross my arms. "Not especially, no." There's a pear tree set in the corner of this room as well, or maybe it's the same one from his cabin, and he just carts it around.

He follows my gaze, and I see it, the moment it clicks, and he realizes I remember. He leans over and whispers something to Everette, who leaves, but not before giving me a look that says he's not done with me yet. Great, now I'm going to regret *not* killing him.

"Have a seat." Sarka points to a chair in front of his desk.

"So I'm a guest now?" I lift my arms slightly to emphasize my dishevelment. I don't feel like a guest. "This all feels so spurious." My tone is formal as I lower myself into the chair. "After all, I'm not here by choice."

"Would you rather I left you in your little pod to suffocate and die?"

"Yes," I say without hesitation. "I'm going to die anyway. I'd rather it be on my own terms." And without casualties, but I don't add that part. I've been saved from imploding, alone in space, only to land in front of this death squad, who are, no doubt, shepherding me to the *Posterus*, where I will take my place in history as the first person to blow up an entire ship with her own body.

He circles his desk and takes a seat across from me. This feels different than my memories. He seems different than I remember, less tightly wound than last time. He's calmer, as if everything he's planned so far has gone his way, and the completion of his mission is inevitable.

"I don't understand why you care so much if we leave. Are you mad they didn't invite you?"

His laughter coats the room like a blanket covering every surface. "What a childish thing to say. You think I'm holding a grudge against the Union? Sulking like a baby because I wasn't invited to your tea party?" His face sobers, and he pulls two glasses down from a cupboard beside his desk. "Have you ever heard of an agave plant?"

I shake my head.

"It used to grow in the southern regions of Earth, Mexico

and some parts of South America. It requires lots of sun and an arid climate to thrive, and so naturally doesn't do so well up here. The sap, when it's fermented and distilled, makes a beverage that is known as liquid gold." Sarka opens a drawer and pulls a glass bottle filled with a soft amber liquid and sets it on the desk in front of me. "Do you know why it's called liquid gold?"

Again, I shake my head.

"Because there is very little of it left in the known universe." He pours a couple fingers in each glass, and when he sets the bottle down, the label is facing me: tequila.

The same stuff Jordan gave me that first night. Now I wonder more than ever where she got her hands on this stuff, liquid gold.

"We are our history. A shared history. And as much as the Union would like to deny it, that history is also our future," says Sarka, taking a slow sip. "It may seem inconsequential to you, but if we leave, if even some of us leave, we are abandoning our history, abandoning who we are as a species."

"I think that's backward and ignorant," I say. "Change has always been feared by those who are too afraid to push forward, to make a sacrifice for the greater good. If we didn't have people like Erikson, or Gagarin or Kita, we wouldn't have progressed as a species. If Erikson hadn't ventured into the unknown, Europeans wouldn't have settled North America. If Gagarin, or any of the early astronauts, hadn't donned spacesuits and blasted into space on a glorified bottle rocket to explore space, we might not have thought it possible. And if Kita hadn't guided that first mission to Mars, we as a species would probably still be stuck on Earth. Extinct. All because it was better to play it safe and stick close to home." I pause, wishing words would get through to him. "This is no different. We're taking the bold step to move into the next phase of human existence, and that requires interstellar travel."

"No. We don't belong out there. Just like this tequila, once the last bottle is drunk, nothing we do will ever bring it back. If we disperse as a species, there is no bringing us back." He pushes a glass toward me.

I shake my head. "Once was enough."

"I assure you, you've not tried tequila before."

I lean forward and inhale. Even that burns my throat. I hack a few times to clear my lungs.

A quick rap on the door halts my impulse to heave the glass of tequila in Sarka's fabricated face. When I turn, the wrinkled woman with a small tablet tucked under her arm slips into the office. She glides silently toward Sarka and hands him the tablet. It's evident he doesn't understand anything on it. He shoves it back into the woman's hands.

"I thought you said she wouldn't remember anything."

The woman's head whips around and her whole body goes rigid. She stalks over to me and pulls me to my feet. I tower over her. She extends weathered hands and cups my face, tugging me lower so she can peer into my eyes. I hover in a half-standing, half-seated position as she assesses me. I feel like a child who's been summoned to the dinner table and made to prove I've washed my hands. "She isn't supposed to remember any of it. The knot releases…a chemical that suppresses her…memories." I have a feeling she's dumbing down much of what she's saying so Sarka understands.

I guess it makes sense that they would want me to forget. They erased all traces of the plasma pulse from the database. The only clue to its theft would be my memories.

"Then how is it she remembers?"

The old woman tilts my head from side to side. Her hands are rough against my skin like she's got tiny burrs on the ends, grappling my cheeks. I'm not exactly sure what she's looking for. Her ebony eyes are very close now, piercing in their intensity. "Did you take anything?"

I nod. “I did.” I don’t think I could lie to those inky eyes even if I wanted to.

She releases my face and pulls from one of her many pockets a small blade. Before I even know what she’s doing or can stop her, she’s grabbed my hand and sliced the tip of my index finger, drawing blood. She places a small smudge of it on another contraption pulled from yet another pocket. She’s holding a small flat rectangle with a screen on one side and a dash of my blood on a dark black pad on the other.

“It put you to sleep?”

I pause because I wouldn’t call what happened to me sleeping.

“You relived it?”

“Yes.” My voice is very quiet, but even so, it appears to reverberate around the room, as if throwing it back in my face. As if the act of admitting it means I belong here; I deserve this. I let it all happen.

She nods, satisfied with my answers and the reading on her device. “Your medical personnel are intelligent.” Her fingers run over the tablet in a rhythm that is both hypnotic and soothing. “They shut down your hippocampus while stimulating your frontal lobe. It allowed your unconscious mind access to them. In a way, reliving the memories as if in a dream state.”

“That sounds nicer than it was,” I say, sucking the blood off my index finger.

Sarka’s eyes droop to the table, and when they come back, there’s a sadness there I can’t explain, edged with anger. “Why would you do that?”

I snort. If I’d known what it was I was remembering, I wouldn’t have bothered. No. That’s not true, I know I would have risked it. Yet I would give anything to forget again.

The old woman leads me to a chair and pushes me down. “Sit,” she says. I wonder how she came to be on this ship, serving the Burrs. Did she volunteer, or was she one of their conquests, taken off a cargo ship in the early years of the Burrs' piracy.

She lifts the hair at the back of my head and prods at the cut. I wince and try to pull away, but she strengthens her grip. "Not infected."

I wonder, and not for the first time, why that should matter. It's as if they're tidying me up for my death. Like the ancient Egyptians who prepared their tombs with bowls of fruit and concubines for their journey to the afterlife.

The intercom buzzes and Everette's breathless voice comes over the speaker. "It's done."

"Excellent." Sarka swipes his hand over his desk and brings up a set of coordinates and energy readouts I don't understand at first. "Have we docked yet?"

"Almost, just need to align with the clamps."

"Is there going to be a problem with that?"

I can hear the sneer in Everette's voice as he says, "No, sir. The new clamps were perfectly aligned."

My stomach drops.

As strong fingers rub a foul-smelling gel on the gash at the back of my head, my mind runs through the sequence of events. A contingency plan. He knew if I found out I would run, and he made sure he'd be able get me back on board, to get his mission back on track. He had me rig our docking clamp for his ship. I want to laugh and cry at the same time. He's brought me back to the *Persephone*.

Sarka turns dark eyes on me. "Time for Plan B."

Chapter Twenty-one

A quick scan of the consoles on the bridge shows me what I already know; Sarka used the plasma pulse to take out the electronics on the *Persephone*. The ship is essentially a dead piece of metal, floating through space until Hartley and his people can get it back up and running again. The red emergency lights cast everything in an ominous glow.

By the time we've taken the bridge, Sarka's crew have infiltrated the ship, taking control of all the key systems, all personnel. The *Persephone* is now under their control.

Several Burrs stand guard, guns raised, watching over the bridge crew. My gaze immediately finds Jordan, who's watching the scene with barely controlled rage.

"Which one of you is the captain?" says Sarka.

Without hesitation, Jordan unfurls from her spot next to Vasa. Her jaw is clamped in anger, her eyes dark slits of fury. There's a bloody gash on the side of her temple, probably from resisting.

Beside me, Sarka's body jerks straight up and becomes stiff. His eyes are the only thing that moves as he traces Jordan's path across the bridge. I wonder if he's had the same reaction I did. She's magnificent in her indignation, and despite my best efforts to remain calm and neutral, my heart picks up a thrilling rhythm as she stalks toward us.

Sarka's voice is oddly dull as he asks her to escort him to her office—which also doubles as her bedroom.

I step between them and say, "Watch him, Captain. He's dangerous."

She crosses her arms and regards him with a bored expression. "I'm well aware of what he's capable of, Ash. I'll be fine."

Jesus, is she trying to intimidate him? If possible, I think this is the one person I've ever met who can't be intimidated. Even my father has had his moments. He usually backed it up with bravado, but I'd seen him waver.

She motions Sarka to lead the way, and I clamp a hand on her wrist and hold her back. "I don't think you should be alone with him."

Her eyes skim over my matted hair, shiner, and the blood on my undershirt visible through the tear in my sweater. There's a brief register of sympathy before she turns back to Sarka, furious. "Seeing as how I'm your commanding officer, I don't really see how you can stop me."

I tighten my grip. "You think I'm worried about rank or a court martial right now?"

Sarka's lips curl in on themselves. "By all means, the more, the merrier. Please lead the way, Alison."

I feel ready to tear into him and rip that smug look from his overly smooth face, but Jordan takes hold of my upper arm and propels me forward. I mentally inventory Jordan's room before we reach it, but since her purge, there's nothing even remotely usable as a weapon. Maybe the globe of Earth could be used to brain him. It's two against one. We might have a chance.

As soon as we reach her office, I have an urge to pull Jordan to me, to make sure she's okay and never let her go. I want to protect her from this, keep her from Sarka and everything that's about to happen. If I had the power, I would send her back to Alpha where she would be safe. But one look at the two of them and I wrap my fists around the extra-long arms of my sweater, keeping my hands to myself. They've staked out separate corners, Sarka behind Jordan's desk, taking the position of power, and Jordan against the wall on the other side of her desk, wary and on edge. There's a familiarity to it that I can't place.

"How noble of you, Alison, to want to protect your captain. But I assure you, I'm not going to hurt her."

"It's not noble. It's my job. I'm expendable. She's not," I say from my corner by the door.

"Ash, I'd hardly call you expendable. No one on this crew is." She folds her arms and casually repositions herself against the wall addressing Sarka, who is eyeing her like she's a caged beast, angry and all claws, capable of anything. "Isn't that right? Everyone serves a purpose."

"And sometimes that purpose is sacrifice."

"You son of a bitch." Jordan's voice is so low and full of menace that it sounds like a growl from deep in her chest.

I cross the room to Jordan. "Hey." I don't really know what else to say. Her breath is strangled in her throat, and she looks like she's ready to lunge across the table and tackle Sarka. I want to comfort her, but I have no idea how. I lay a gentle hand on her arm. There's something else besides anger in her expression; there's a hatred I can't explain. She's always been a defender of the Burrs, so much so that I've often wondered how she can see them as human and not the monsters everyone else does.

"It's okay," I say. Our eyes meet, and all the fear and uncertainty I'm feeling fades away. There's just those dark blue eyes locked on mine. I have an urge to take her face in my hands, to soothe her fears, ease all her hurt.

Too soon she breaks contact. She laughs. It's not the usual musical sound that fills the room and my mind, it's bitter and flat. "He's going to force you, one way or another, to kill forty-five thousand people and destroy decades of work and 'it's okay'?" She rips her arm from my grasp. "He's going to kill you, Ash! He's going to kill all of us, and for what purpose? An ideal."

She faces Sarka, her hands planted on her desk, leaning toward him, practically spitting with fury. "An ideal that should've died decades ago with you and your kind." She turns, addressing this next part to me. "Do you know what he thinks will happen if we leave the solar system? He actually thinks we will cease to be human, that our humanity is wrapped up in these particular stars and this particular sun. He thinks that we will no longer be a unified species." Her fists clench and the knuckles become white, then a blotchy red. "And to think that you," she points to Sarka, "you of all people believe that what you do can be called unity or humane. It's for this very reason we should leave. Leave your antiquated ideals behind."

There's a flash, just a brief scowl, on Sarka's face, then his lips turn up at the end, and the amusement is back. He plops down in her chair, noticing something behind me. Our eyes meet, and there's a twinkle there. I'm not entirely sure what it means. He turns his attention back to Jordan. "You won't mind dying for the cause, will you, sweetheart? After all, you've already died once for it."

Before I can even begin to guess what he means by that, he's up again, angling across the desk, reaching for something on the shelf next to me. "And Alison here, well, she understands. I'm sure she'll give her life for the cause." He pulls down the bottle of tequila. "She's already given so much of herself to it already."

I anticipate Jordan's dive, snaking my arm around her waist before she's able to reach for Sarka. He's just trying to get a rise out of us, or more specifically, Jordan. I shouldn't be so calm, but I am.

"Always a temper, but then, you didn't get that from me. You should take lessons from Alison here; she's been a model guest. Although Everette might not agree. He lost two fingers."

"It should've been more." I fold my arms across my breasts, not sorry in the least. "He has problems keeping them to himself."

I scrunch my eyes as the image of Everette charging at me

comes back. My nostrils flare, and the scent of apricots is replaced by the stench of soil and fish and dung. And suddenly I'm back in that cell, throttling Everette with my chains. The odor of our sweat, the sound of his fingers popping like sausages between the chains, it all crowds into my mind.

I need distance, from the pity on Jordan's face and the barrage of emotions sluicing through me at this moment. I retreat to Jordan's bed, collapsing on the firm mattress to watch the duel between Sarka and Jordan. I hear raised voices, a mixture of baritone and alto ascending from across the desk. And it hits me, what's so familiar about this. They remind me of my father and me, a thousand arguments combined as one. My own petulant, headstrong, stubborn ego fighting against the bravado of someone who's held his own against the Commons and Union fleet leaders. In truth, my father and I will always butt heads; we're too similar not to. The phrase my mom used to use was that we were cut from the same cloth. I'd like to think that if it was the same cloth, mine had a bolder design.

And then the tail end of their argument filters through.

"Mom's dead, leave it be." Jordan's voice is low, only a rasp; the threat is unmistakable.

"Just like you were? I think I'll take the chance and see for myself." His gaze falls on the sweatshirt strewn on the bed next to me. "Delta Academy? That's a good place to start."

"If you go anywhere near Delta, I'll hunt you down and—"

"And what? Pout at me? Jordan, sit down. Let's talk about this like grownups." And just like that, I'm gutted. I can see it so plainly. I don't know how I missed it before. Davis Sarka is Jordan's father. Even with all Sarka's surgeries, there's no mistaking the eyes and nose and jut of their stubborn jaws.

I jump off the bed. "What the fuck?"

They both stop and stare as if I've just risen from the dead.

Just then, a voice cuts in over the intercom. I recognize it as Everette's and shudder.

"Sir, we've found the engineer."

"Good. I'll be there in a second." Sarka strides toward the door, opens it, and speaks in a low voice to one of his men. He comes back with one set of shackles and grabs Jordan's arm before she can pull away, then captures her wrist with the metal bracelet. It snaps shut. He then turns to me. "Alison." He motions for me to come forward. I freeze. A million things run through my mind. One is how much it will hurt if I charge him. I'm still in bare feet, and there's not much I can do in an attack against a man who probably is double my weight. But I should try.

Sarka shakes his head, reading my thoughts. It's uncanny how he always seems to know what I'm thinking. "Don't try it, Alison. I have two armed guards outside in the hall. It will not be pleasant if I have to use force against you."

I don't move. He's found the engineer. I know he means Hartley. They're going to make him get the ship back up and running. We're still a few hours from the *Posterus*. There's a lot I can do with a few hours, but will I get the chance? Over forty-five thousand people are waiting to welcome us and the new engine that will carry a quarter of the species to a new home.

Then a hopelessness descends. What will happen if the Burrs succeed and we do blow up the *Posterus*, will they attempt another generational ship? Will they still try to find humans a new home? Or did we just spend the better part of two decades building a ship that will lead us nowhere? *No!*

Sarka's patience has finally thinned. He yanks hard on Jordan's arm, pulling her with him as he stomps toward me. I'm startled out of my thoughts. He has a tight grip on my wrist before I'm able to pull free. Shit. It clicks into place, sending a shudder down my spine. I peer at our restraints. They're locked with a passcode, which makes them almost impossible to break out of. Almost.

He brushes the back of his hands over my cheek. I pull away from the soft touch, but he tangles his hand in my hair, pulling me close enough to see the stubble on his chin, to smell his breath, which reeks of pears. "Don't do it, Alison. I know you. This is not an opportunity to plan your escape." He releases me and taps the side of my head. "I know you. Remember that." And with those parting words, he leaves, locking Jordan and me in her cabin.

CHAPTER TWENTY-TWO

As soon as we're alone in Jordan's cabin, she turns to me. "Oh, Ash, what did they do to you?" Her fingertips trace the tender skin below my eye. I pull away, a little harsher than I intend.

I tilt her head. The gash on her temple has crusted over, but the smeared blood makes it appear worse than it is. My anxiety lessens a little. "I'm so sorry. I never meant for any of this to happen."

She wraps her hand around my wrist, eyes locked on mine. "He was following in our wake. I had Vasa keep an eye out for their emissions. There was nothing you could do to stop him. He still would've taken the ship if you had stayed on board. I should've told you in the pod, but I panicked." She shakes her head and drops her gaze. "I have a tendency to do that around you."

I love that she admits this, and the only thing I want to do is close the space between us, to feel comfort in the heat of her body. All it would take is a simple nudge at the small of her back to make that happen. She bites her lip and peers back at me, and I know in that look she would follow me. But instead, I take a step back and pull my wrist from her hand. There's too much I need explained.

"How is Davis Sarka your father?" I ask.

"Don't make me explain the birds and the bees to you, Ash. I don't think I have the patience for it."

"That's not what I meant, and you know it." I steer her toward the bed. The chain on the restraints jangles as I pull her next to me. "How is it possible that Sarka's your father? I thought you grew up on Delta."

She nods, but doesn't look at me. Instead she studies our hands resting in shackles next to each other on the bed. The dark metal stands stark against our pale skin, orbiting our wrists like the moon does the Earth. She entwines our fingers, and when she raises her head, resignation clouds her deep blue eyes. "You want the long version or the short version?"

"Let's save the extended version for when we have more time."

She sweeps her hair back, taking care to free several strands that have become stuck in the blood on her temple, then turns to look out the windows at the stars dotting the view. "My mom was born on Delta. She was second generation to be born on the Belt. The way she explained it, things were a lot different back then. The Commons wasn't as powerful as it is now, and Union fleet was in its infancy. There, um…there wasn't as much hostility between the early Belt settlements then. It was still very much a joint effort. And the Burrs hadn't become as organized, they were still just leftovers from an almost forgotten war. When my mom turned eighteen, she enlisted in Union fleet. She said she wanted to explore, and the idea of spending the rest of her life farming and milking cows on Delta was only a step up from digging for minerals in the mines on Eps."

"Sounds like you had a similar experience."

"I think I would've rather lost a limb than stick around there." Jordan huffs, raising her left arm to emphasize which limb she'd be willing to sacrifice. "I mean, it wasn't a bad way to grow up. I just didn't want to do it for life. My mom knew what would happen to her just as much as I did. Marriage, babies, an early death from backbreaking work. That wasn't for her. She'd only been in service for two years before she went missing and was eventually declared dead, at least that's what her service record says. I looked it up as soon as I had enough clearance." This last part is spoken into her chest. It's so quiet, as if she's ashamed of how she found out. Before I can say anything, she clears her throat and continues.

"My mom was a breathtaking woman. She was taller than most of the women on the station. I remember she would carry herself with such confidence, as if the surrounding filth couldn't touch her. I wanted to be like that someday. Her beauty saved her life when the ship was raided by the Burrs, just a few million kilometers from Earth's moon. Most of the crew were killed, but the captain took a liking to her and let her live. He took her to their home base, a patchwork space station that orbits Earth. It's ancient. Parts of it date back to before artificial gravity. They would float through modules like they were swimming underwater. I can't imagine they're still using it, but that's where I was born. It's where I spent the first twelve years of my life, looking down on Earth, wanting what I couldn't have."

"I know," I say. And I do know this feeling so well.

"Earth always seemed so close, and yet, it was this intangible fantasy. This orbiting body, full of adventures and mystique."

I nod and squeeze her hand, letting her know I understand.

"To me, it represented the life I should have had. But I was always stuck looking down, forever removed from it." She stops, her gaze landing on the globe of Earth sitting on her shelf.

"You don't have to tell me any more if it's too difficult."

She shakes her head. "I want you to know." Her voice is soft and a little husky. Her thumb traces the lines along my palm. It grabs at me in places that aren't appropriate for the heaviness of the moment. "She, um, lived with them for about a year and a half before she became pregnant with me. The way he would tell it, they fell in love. But I think it was just survival on her part.

"I was eight when she started planning our escape. At that age I still lived in blissful ignorance. I remember being proud of my father. Everyone looked up to him. They listened when he spoke. At the time, I didn't realize it was fear that made them do it."

I nod. When I was young, I used to watch my father address the Commons from the sidelines, in awe at the way he could command a room.

"I didn't understand a lot of things," she says. "One day I followed him down to the lower parts of the station where I knew I wasn't supposed to go, but that only made it all the more appealing. It was the screams that drew me." She stops for a long moment, her eyes scrunching tight, remembering something long forgotten.

I look away, remembering my own time aboard Sarka's ship. I don't want Jordan to see the dread that's suddenly crept into my every pore.

"The man was bound to a chair, his wrists tied to the armrests. My father had a knife, which he was pushing into the man's nail bed." She opens her eyes, directing them toward me. "Is that what he did to you?"

I try to find a neutral expression before turning to face her. "Jordan, I'm not going to tell you what he did to me."

"Because it's worse?"

"No, because it's over. It happened. It's done. And nothing I do or say will change that. I don't want you to know what he did because if you do, it'll make it real." And if I relive it, I won't be as strong as I need to be for her.

"Jesus, Ash. Don't say things like that. It's just going to make me think the worst."

I realize all I want to do is protect her, which is bizarre. After all, she grew up with him. Who better to know the evil of what the Burrs do than her?

I stroke the back of her hand. "I'm okay, Jordan, really. What happened after?"

It takes a moment for her to understand what I'm asking. But she does eventually continue. "I think my mom realized that I'd never have a real childhood if we stayed. All these years later, I don't know how she managed to get us out of there. At the time, I was oblivious. She was always good at keeping a buffer between me and what happened on the station.

"When they'd had a successful raid the crew would parade down the main corridor with their spoils, which often included people. My mom would always make sure I was safely in our rooms whenever that happened, but I'd hear the other kids talk about it. My mother would've been paraded like a prize Sarka had won. As a kid, I remember being sorry that I never got to see it, but now I can't imagine what it would feel like, being gawked at and appraised like an object, something to be traded. The humiliation she must have felt.

"It was early morning, the day we escaped. I was still asleep, and she woke me up. I still remember the feel of her hand clamped over my mouth as she told me to quietly pack up only the essentials." Jordan laughs a little. "My idea of essentials at twelve left much to be desired. I stuffed my bag with trinkets, prized possessions, a few picture books, shells, all my treasures from Earth." She points to the globe on the shelf. "The last thing I grabbed was that bottle of tequila. I wanted something to remember my dad. It was his favorite, and I thought if I had one of his treasures he'd never forget about me. The concept of forever back then wasn't as easy to grasp. Time has a way of being smaller when you're little, you know?"

I press my forehead to hers. "Time has a way of becoming the exact opposite of what you need at any given moment."

We breathe together like this for a minute or two, and I know she understands what I'm really saying. "Life for me hadn't been so bad." She pulls away. "I followed my mom because I loved her, but I remember being terrified to leave. I had friends and people I loved. I couldn't understand how my mom could just give it all up. I didn't realize what life must have been like for her.

"We boarded a small vessel with two other families, both like my mom and me, women who had been captured and claimed by two Burrs. There were seven of us in total. Most of the fleet were on a raiding mission, so there wasn't a lot of security watching. The plan was to rendezvous with a cargo ship once we were clear of Earth's moon, but we were intercepted by Union fleet, and naturally they assumed we were a raiding party.

"My mom and I made it to an escape pod. Some of the other families weren't so lucky. Only one other family managed to escape, a little boy and his mother. We spent almost four days in the pod. My mom had given me something to knock me out so I wouldn't use so much oxygen. I woke up in the cargo ship med center. She had taken something after I'd fallen asleep. They said it was painless. She wanted to make sure I had enough air to survive until rescue came. There wouldn't have been enough for both of us."

There's no way I can watch the look of sheer anguish on her face. I lean into her; it's the only comfort I can give, the way we're shackled together. It's nice to see the real Jordan again. It occurs to me that it's the only time she ever shows any genuine emotion, like in the med center with the diagnostic cube, I get glimpses of what she's really feeling when she drops her shield. We stay like that for several long moments, the warmth of her body seeping into mine. I try to keep my thoughts on Jordan as a child instead of Jordan the woman molded against my body.

I get why she'll never see the Burrs as monsters. She may see what they do now through the eyes of an adult, but her memories of her dad, of Sarka, are through the eyes of a child. Part of how she sees him in her past must be mixed up with that unconditional love. I remember when the awe of watching my father speak to the Commons began to crumble. The moment I was old enough to understand what he was actually saying and that I didn't agree with him.

She pulls back, taking all the warmth of her body with her. "Nobody knows that Sarka's my father, not even Katherine, my mom's friend, who raised me."

"And no one ever has to. I won't say anything."

She leans her forehead against mine. "What do you think the odds of us getting out of here alive are?"

"Slim." Sarka's voice startles us both.

Jordan jerks away from me.

Sarka drops a uniform on the edge of Jordan's bed. "It's time," he says.

At my dumbfounded look, he explains. "We can't have you escorting Hartley to the engine room on the *Posterus* wearing one of our uniforms, can we?" I want to punch the grotesque grin off his face. He bends between us to enter the code on our restraints and removes them.

When I still don't move, he says, "Come now, Alison. Don't be shy. It's nothing I haven't seen before." He peers over at Jordan, his grin widening. "Or should I amend that to, nothing *we* haven't seen before."

It only takes a moment for the mortification to fade from Jordan's face. It's replaced by understanding and what he's implying, that *he's* seen me naked. She launches off the bed toward him.

Chapter Twenty-three

I'm escorted executioner style down the corridors of the *Persephone* toward the air dock where I'll meet Hartley and the new engine core to board the *Posterus*. I should be panicking, but for the first time in weeks my mind is still. Perhaps it's because for the first time since I stepped across Jordan's threshold, I know how she feels and I'm more certain than ever that what I do next will be to protect her, even if I am breaking a promise.

Watching her fly at Sarka, my mind formulated a plan. Her attempt to launch herself at Sarka, however ill-advised, was easily deflected. He was expecting that response, hoping for it. But instead of being triumphant, as he caught her in an easy choke hold, a strange bitterness seeped through his composure. What does he resent, I wonder, that the woman he supposedly loved deserted him, taking his daughter with her? Or is it that he's required to hurt his daughter, both physically and emotionally, to accomplish his goals? In the end, it doesn't matter. He will do what's needed to finish what he's started. And all I can do is what I do so well, apparently—put myself in harm's way to protect those around me. I will never know if I've succeeded.

Hartley is standing by the air dock. It's obvious they haven't filled him in on anything because when he sees me, his eyes expand and his mouth drops open. "Ash!" he cries. "Where did you come from? I heard you left the ship."

I wave the comment off as I approach. I'm now dressed in my uniform, neatly pressed and smelling of cleaning solution. A faint floral scent wafts off me in waves. I notice that because since leaving Jordan, everything is enhanced—colors, sounds, and odors.

"What's going on? They won't tell me anything." He's holding on to the engine core with tight fingers, afraid someone will take it from him, like ripping a security blanket from the arms of a child. Hartley likes order, and this new plan—so last minute—must be killing him.

I'm not about to tell him anything in front of Sarka's men. I don't want them to realize how much I know. "They asked me to escort you to the engine room on the *Posterus*."

Hartley nods and his face smooths with relief. I guess he thinks he's safe with me. And now I realize Dr. Prashad didn't tell him anything about the nanobots clinging to his innards like freeloaders looking for a ride. He has no idea what's about to happen, and I don't have the heart to tell him he's about to die. But in order for my plan to work, that's what needs to happen. Hartley has never struck me as the self-sacrifice type. I can't risk filling him in and hoping he's an eager participant. But if Sarka has his way, we'll all be dead anyway.

As soon as Hartley starts the core, the flare will arc, and I will act as the spark to ignite Hartley. Even if I can't resist any suggestions from my knot, it might not matter how far I am from him. The amount of energy coursing through the room at that point should be enough of a catalyst to set him off. The explosion will be devastating to anyone aboard the *Posterus* and all vessels connected at the air docks. Which means Sarka is sacrificing himself and Jordan. To disengage would only draw attention to the *Persephone* and his plan. Unless he's planning on using an escape pod and has his ship waiting on the periphery.

I keep my mouth shut. I know Hartley won't appreciate his

sacrifice, but the forty-five thousand people aboard the *Posterus* will.

"Let's go," I say, pointing toward the open dock. Just beyond, I can see the bustle of people in the corridors of the docking station. Hartley tugs the container, and it glides along behind him as he makes his way through the port.

Growing up, I'd heard so much about the *Posterus* and all her innovations, but I've only ever seen 3-D renderings. This will be like stepping through the looking glass and discovering an imaginary world turned to reality. The ship was designed to be an amazing flying bio-station, long-term and self-sustaining. It grows, maintains, and recycles its own food supply. We can harvest and create water on the fly, and all our energy is from renewable sources.

Hartley and I report first to the station manager to let him know that we've arrived and will need an internal escort to the engine room. Hartley fidgets with one of the case clamps with a nervous energy I've come to expect from him. He scratches at his beard, and for the first time, I take a good look at him. He's exhausted. The sallow pouches of skin under his eyes sag, and his skin is dry and flaky. I kick the container to get his attention, and when I have it, I give him a look that silently asks if he's okay. He nods. It's a sharp movement, and just as soon his gaze moves toward the activity beyond. I empathize. I haven't slept in what feels like days. My eyes feel as if they want to drop from my face and look for someone else who will treat them better.

I need him present. I need us to make it to the engine room. For my plan to work, we have to go through with this. If for any reason we divert, Sarka has promised me that Jordan will die. I can still feel his breath on my ear at the whispered exchange as I left her cabin. I don't doubt his sincerity that her death would be excruciatingly slow and painful.

The station manager points us toward a behemoth of a man

standing at the entrance to the main throughway of the ship. He's dressed in the green uniform of the *Posterus* crew and has short, cropped hair and a square jaw. He must be part of the engineering team that will help us install the engine core. Originally Hartley was to have our crew help, but Sarka had Jordan send a message saying we will do it with a much smaller team.

I approach the engineer, wondering if he's going to salute or shake my hand. If he were Union fleet, protocol would require him to salute, but seeing as he's part of the *Posterus* crew, he isn't required to. He smiles at me and gives me an informal salute and then holds out his hand. I shake it quickly and smile tightly.

"Lieutenant Ash?" he asks, and I nod. "I'm Amit. It's good to meet you. Welcome to the *Posterus*." Then his eyes focus on the man beside me, and I've lost him because Hartley has another geekling to add to his collection.

The man's hand shakes as he reaches for Hartley. "It is an honor to meet you, Dr. Hartley." I almost laugh at the title. But the fawning is good for Hartley, as he loses some of his nervousness and puffs slightly at the praise.

"Lead the way," I say, stepping on the main concourse of the *Posterus*, and then stop, as all my attention is pulled short at the sight that greets me. The concourse is massive, and even that isn't doing it justice. The corridor is probably half a kilometer wide and at least two long. It stretches above us to the windowed ceiling, showing a smattering of stars beyond the thick metallic glass. On either side, office and cabin windows overlook the concourse. Everything is integrated in both form and purpose. Edible plants line one side of the wall, forming part of our food chain, aiding in filtering out carbon dioxide, and adding to the aesthetic of the concourse.

Hartley slaps me on the back. "Don't forget to breathe, Lieutenant." He winks at me, and I wonder where this sudden confidence comes from. A second ago he looked like he was going to burst into tears.

"Hartley, I hope you've brought some Jackies. I think we're going to need them."

He nods, and I know he's prepared for a number of contingencies.

We follow Amit as he weaves and skirts groups of people milling about. It really is like walking through a city. There are markets and shops where people can barter and trade for goods. We pass several commissaries full of people eating, laughing, talking. I've never seen anything to rival it, not even Alpha, and that biosphere is easily the most impressive of all the human settlements on the Belt. Seeing it like this, my resolve hardens. I can't let Sarka destroy this. It is the ultimate in human ingenuity. On the Belt, we have the asteroids to mine and pull resources from. We have the unflagging solar energy from the sun. But once we begin our journey, we're on our own. We will have to mine asteroids as we go, collecting water and other valuable resources en route. But more importantly, we will have to problem solve on the fly. There are a million things that can go wrong, and we won't know all of them. No one can possibly predict every possible outcome. And only once we're out there will we know whether we planned for enough contingencies to make it. This is our future. Despite the turmoil inside I can't help but feel the excitement, the energy within everyone I pass. It crackles like a live connection stringing everyone together. Every single person aboard this ship is making history. We are all Erikson, Gagarin, and Kita in one, ready to brave the unknown, not because we can, or even because we should, but because we must.

Amit and Hartley are deep in conversation ahead of me. Every now and then Amit will raise his voice and turn to include me in the tour he's giving. It takes a few moments to shift his whole body, turning as if his head is fused with his shoulders. I nod but don't actually hear what he's saying. As we get closer to our destination, my mind becomes focused on my goal, and everything else fades away, all my fears, all my emotions, leaving the all-consuming need to succeed.

We enter a lift and descend to the bowels of the ship. It's less elegant the farther down we go, but no less impressive. The sleek design has been replaced with more functional and lightweight components, but the grandeur, the massive scale is still there. The lift's windows reveal myriad worlds. Like a honeycomb, each is self-contained, yet part of a larger whole. We exit the lift and enter the engine room, which is almost as grand as the main concourse—almost. There are no windows of any kind, but the ceiling is easily five decks high, with open corridors housing computer banks along the edges of the room. In the center is the well for the core. A hydraulic arm is suspended above the pit to lift and position the core into place.

I stop at the entrance and take stock. There are a few engineers scattered at various workstations around the room, no more than six people. My first priority is to get them out. I haven't figured out how yet. We'll need help getting the engine core into place, and I don't know how long that will take.

"Amit, do you mind if I speak with Hartley alone for a second?"

"Of course, take all the time you need. I'll be over here briefing my people. When you're done come find me."

Amit plods toward central control, where he's swarmed by green-clad engineers, like worker bees waiting for their orders. He towers over them and speaks in a low rumble, giving orders. A few steal glances our way.

I motion for Hartley to follow me over to the control panel, scanning it for what I need. I bring up a couple of screens and then add a shortcut so I can regain access to that menu as quickly as possible later. Hartley is watching me, and his eyes grow wide, missing nothing that I've just done.

"Lieutenant, why do I have the feeling I've been left in the dark here?"

I try to ignore the growing panic in his voice and keep mine calm. "What exactly were you told, Hartley?"

He opens up a menu on the panel in front of him and reviews several procedures. Without even waiting, he's started the initialization sequence. "I was told I would be using the team from the *Posterus* to install the engine core instead of my own. I don't like it, Ash. Why did they decide to keep my guys out of it? We've been setting up protocols all week." He turns to me, and I can see his brain working through the events of the last couple of days, trying to piece it all together.

"Who told you that?"

"One of the Burrs. They said they were coming with us, that they weren't going to be left behind."

Huh. Smooth. Hartley will be more likely to play along if he thinks they just want a ride. He has no idea he's about to help blow this whole place to bits. I close my eyes, wondering if I should just tell him. Instead, I think back to Jordan's cabin. Before I left, she grabbed my arm and made me promise not to do anything stupid. I can still feel the tender brush of her thumb against my wrist, though I wish I could forget. It makes what I have to do next all the more difficult. I see Jordan's eyes, intense and dark, staring into mine, urging me to promise to be careful. It's an easy lie, and I tell it well.

CHAPTER TWENTY-FOUR

"Hartley, I need you to listen carefully and do exactly what I say."

His curious gaze follows the direction of my finger pointed at his chest.

"Exactly, okay?"

He steps toward me, and I take a step back. I don't want to risk touching him. I pull the restraints from my cargo pocket. I grabbed them off the bed when Sarka had his back to me. I hand them to Hartley. Step one, make sure I can't get near Hartley.

"I need you to cuff me to this console. Choose a new combination for the lock, one I won't know. And then I need you to bring me a Jackie, but set it down so I can reach it if I need to." As I speak, the frown on Hartley's face deepens. Now I know he's scared—there's no inappropriate comments about restraints and bondage. This is all too much for him. I'll be lucky if I can get him to focus for more than a minute. What should have been a triumphant, life goal moment has been stolen from him, and his confusion is quickly turning to suspicion.

"What's really going on, Lieutenant? What do you need the Jackie for? Those things can kill you if you don't know how to handle them properly." He pulls out a set of work gloves and shoves them toward me. "Here, at least take some safety gloves."

I snatch the gloves from Hartley and stuff them in my cargo

pocket. I won't need them. The whole point of having the Jackie is to overload my system, so Hartley doesn't.

When I first discovered the Jackies, I was furious. Instead of working on the *Persephone*'s new hardware upgrades, Hartley was dicking around on something that not only appeared useless, but dangerous. One touch and a hundred amps course through your body, enough to kill anyone, even someone as large as Amit. Let's hope I have the guts to use it.

Hartley is staring at me, all bug-eyed. His fingers are twisting themselves into a knot, and his hairline has become slick with sweat. He's about five seconds from bolting.

"The Burrs aren't coming with us—"

"If they want to come, I say let them." He swipes at his forehead with his arm, causing the hairs in the front to stick out in odd directions.

"They have no intention of letting us get out of this solar system." I point to his back. "I wasn't trying to kill you when I stabbed you."

"I know, Ash. It was the mind knot that made you do it. I don't hold that against you." His expression is so understanding and open that I actually believe he's forgiven me.

"That's not what I mean," I say. "The Burrs didn't want you dead, and that's not why they had me stab you. It was a cover. I was lacing you with nanobots. You're as combustible as a dead pine tree soaked in gasoline." I thrust my arm toward him. "When you cuff me, don't touch my skin, okay?"

"I'm not going to cuff you, Ash. What's really going on?" He hesitates, then lowers his voice, even though he's already talking so low, I can barely hear him. "Is this you talking, or the mind knot?"

"Hartley, just cuff me to the goddamned console already."

"But why? What happens after I do that?" He's edging away from me now. If I don't get him on board quickly, he's going to bolt.

"The Burrs are trying to sabotage the mission. They want to blow up your engine."

He's shaking his head now, and I'm worried I've lost him. He's got this look on his face, the one people get when they're wondering just how crazy you really are. I can see the inner fight he's having with himself, weighing how likely it is that I'm lying with how likely it is that the Burrs would want to destroy his precious engine. He peers over at Amit, who's still conferring with the six engineers off to the side. He looks over at us, and I wave to let Amit know everything's fine—although it makes me appear even more insane.

"You're nuts, Ash. You know that?" Hartley says.

"Hartley, I may be a lot of things, but you know I would never put anyone but myself at risk. I need you to trust me, a lot of lives depend on what you do in the next five minutes. And if you don't want to believe me, I understand. All I ask is that you leave the engine room and let me do this."

"What are you going to do?"

I take a deep breath. *Here we go.* "Eject the core." Since the system is in place to protect the ship, the core will be well out of range by the time we explode.

"From in here? You'll suck us all out! It'll take months to find the engine core and repair it!" His volume is getting higher with each syllable. "You can't do that—"

"Keep your voice down." Amit is starting toward us with the group of engineers following closely. "Are you in or out?"

His gaze shifts to the well beside us.

"Hartley, there are forty-five thousand people on board this ship. There are only nine people in this engine room. Do the math. You want to be a hero or a fucking idiot?" I watch him agonize over it. There really is no decision, not when you factor in the numbers. I guess he's deciding whether to stay or go.

"Jesus, Ash."

"Hartley, there are only two outcomes. Mine at least saves

the engine." And the ship, and thousands of lives, but this is Hartley. I have to appeal to what he really cares about.

His eyes bore into mine, and I see his choice. I've said the right thing. That engine is like his firstborn. "Fine, I'll help. But just for the record, I wish I'd never met you. I better get something named after me."

I let the breath I've been holding out. "I bet they name the engine after you."

"I don't need to blow up for them to do that. I invented the damn thing."

The next few moments turn slowly, feeling like hours instead of minutes. I've given up trying to think of a way to get the engineers out. Anything I can think of would be too suspicious.

As I wait, I think of Jordan and every little part that had me so drawn to her. From the moment we met. Her fruit-laced scent, her ivory skin, her inky hair. That determined look. But most of all, her strength. My mind flits from one moment to the next, the way the water glistened off her eyelashes in the shower, the feel of her strong thighs wrapped around me in the pod. It breaks my heart, all the moments we'll never share now. But it's because of these next few moments that she'll live, and these sacrifices are the only way to make that happen. She's the only person I ever truly felt a connection with. There was just something about the way she looked at me, like she was seeing past the surface, past the bravado, and really seeing me, with all our differences and similarities. She, better than anyone, understands my struggle to break free from my father's shadow, and that it doesn't define me, but makes me stronger. It made us stronger. And even though I never said the words, I love her. And for the first time in my life, I know, without having to ask, without having to hear it, that she feels it, too. It's this thought, more than anything, more than duty or responsibility, that gives me the determination to complete this task. And deep down, one day, I know she'll understand.

It takes another ten minutes to connect the engine to the

hydraulic arm and another twenty to lift it into place. *Focus.* The actual initialization process is what will take the longest. It'll take at least two weeks to integrate it into all the ship's systems, but we're not expecting to keep the engine that long. I don't suspect we have too much longer. There's a hum beginning underneath my skin. I'm not sure if it's mental anticipation or something else, something more dangerous.

I'm doing the right thing. No more thoughts.

As soon as we have a moment alone, I tell Hartley to connect me to the console and leave. He slides a Jackie along the ground next to me but shakes his head.

"You need two people to eject the core, didn't you see the protocol? Besides, they won't name shit after me if I live through this."

I smile at him. If you'd asked me two weeks ago whether I thought Hartley was capable of this, I would have said no. Hell, half an hour ago, I would have said no.

Just then, the ship rocks, banking us to the port side, and sending Hartley and me to the ground. The Jackie slides and drops into the well and I stupidly reach and grab for it. When my hand connects, my whole consciousness explodes into a million pieces before reassembling. My arms and legs buzz with electricity as one hundred amps surge through my system.

Vaguely I hear Amit shout, "What the hell was that?" I can't move. Instead I'm lying on the ground, my hand still fused with the Jackie.

Hartley pulls himself up. His fingers fly over the console. "I don't have any access to the sensors from here."

Amit pushes him to the side. "You won't, not down here. Only the bridge or the main command center will have access to the sensors."

The ship rocks again, and I slide closer to the well. In my head, I'm screaming, but nothing comes out of my mouth.

"Are we under attack?" asks Hartley. He must be wondering

the same thing I am: Either Union fleet got word of the Burrs' interference, or we're being attacked by Burrs. Maybe they thought things weren't progressing fast enough.

"The bridge is still trying to figure out what's going on," says Amit. "There aren't any other ships in the area. We couldn't be under attack."

Two of the engineers continue to pore over the data from the displays in front of them, running over and illuminating every possibility from stabilization errors to hull breach.

This is it.

Without thinking, Hartley reaches down to grab me before I go over. His hand connects with my arm—and I wish it was Jordan, but that will never happen now.

The engine core rocks in the cradle of the hydraulic arm. We've run out of time.

We tip once more, and this time I begin to slip over the edge into the well.

I hear nothing.

I see nothing.

Everything goes white. The feeling of nothingness washes over me.

About the Author

CJ Birch works and lives in Toronto with her partner Kim and a growing collection of dependants. When not writing or devouring books, she works as a video editor for television. A lover of words, coffee (the really strong kind that seeps from your pores announcing, by smell alone, your obsession), and sarcasm. *Unknown Horizons* is her first novel.

Books Available From Bold Strokes Books

Escape in Time by Robyn Nyx. Working in the past is hell on your future. (978-1-62639-855-9)

Forget-Me-Not by Kris Bryant. Is love worth walking away from the only life you've ever dreamed of? (978-1-62639-865-8)

Highland Fling by Anna Larner. On vacation in the Scottish Highlands, Eve Eddison falls for the enigmatic forestry officer Moira Burns despite Eve's best friend's campaign to convince her that Moira will break her heart. (978-1-62639-853-5)

Phoenix Rising by Rebecca Harwell. As Storm's Quarry faces invasion from a powerful neighbor, a mysterious newcomer with powers equal to Nadya's challenges everything she believes about herself and her future. (978-1-62639-913-6)

Soul Survivor by I. Beacham. Sam and Joey have given up on hope, but when fate brings them together it gives them a chance to change each other's life and make dreams come true. (978-1-62639-882-5)

Strawberry Summer by Melissa Brayden. When Margaret Beringer's first love Courtney Carrington returns to their small town, she must grapple with their troubled past and fight the temptation for a very delicious future. (978-1-62639-867-2)

The Girl on the Edge of Summer by J.M. Redmann. Micky Knight accepts two cases, but neither is the easy investigation it appears. The past is never past—and young girls lead complicated, even dangerous lives. (978-1-62639-687-6)

Unknown Horizons by CJ Birch. The moment Lieutenant Alison Ash steps aboard the *Persephone*, she knows her life will never be the same. (978-1-62639-938-9)

The Sniper's Kiss by Justine Saracen. The power of a kiss: it can swell your heart with splendor, declare abject submission, and sometimes blow your brains out. (978-1-62639-839-9)

Divided Nation, United Hearts by Yolanda Wallace. In a nation torn in two by a most uncivil war, can love conquer the divide? (978-1-62639-847-4)

Fury's Bridge by Brey Willows. What if your life depended on someone who didn't believe in your existence? (978-1-62639-841-2)

Lightning Strikes by Cass Sellars. When Parker Duncan and Sydney Hyatt's one-night stand turns to more, both women must fight demons past and present to cling to the relationship neither of them thought she wanted. (978-1-62639-956-3)

Love in Disaster by Charlotte Greene. A professor and a celebrity chef are drawn together by chance, but can their attraction survive a natural disaster? (978-1-62639-885-6)

Secret Hearts by Radclyffe. Can two women from different worlds find common ground while fighting their secret desires? (978-1-62639-932-7)

Sins of Our Fathers by A. Rose Mathieu. Solving gruesome murder cases is only one of Elizabeth Campbell's challenges; another is her growing attraction to the female detective who is hell-bent on keeping her client in prison. (978-1-62639-873-3)

Troop 18 by Jessica L. Webb. Charged with uncovering the destructive secret that a troop of RCMP cadets has been hiding, Andy must put aside her worries about Kate and uncover the conspiracy before it's too late. (978-1-62639-934-1)

Worthy of Trust and Confidence by Kara A. McLeod. FBI Special Agent Ryan O'Connor is about to discover the hard way that when you can only handle one type of answer to a question, it really is better not to ask. (978-1-62639-889-4)

Amounting to Nothing by Karis Walsh. When mounted police officer Billie Mitchell steps in to save beautiful murder witness Merissa Karr, worlds collide on the rough city streets of Tacoma, Washington. (978-1-62639-728-6)

Becoming You by Michelle Grubb. Airlie Porter has a secret. A deep, dark, destructive secret that threatens to engulf her if she can't find the courage to face who she really is and who she really wants to be with. (978-1-62639-811-5)

Birthright by Missouri Vaun. When spies bring news that a swordswoman imprisoned in a neighboring kingdom bears the Royal mark, Princess Kathryn sets out to rescue Aiden, true heir to the Belstaff throne. (978-1-62639-485-8)

Crescent City Confidential by Aurora Rey. When romance and danger are in the air, writer Sam Torres learns the Big Easy is anything but. (978-1-62639-764-4)

Love Down Under by MJ Williamz. Wylie loves Amarina, but if Amarina isn't out, can their relationship last? (978-1-62639-726-2)

Privacy Glass by Missouri Vaun. Things heat up when Nash Wiley commandeers a limo and her best friend for a late drive out to the beach: Champagne on ice, seat belts optional, and privacy glass a must. (978-1-62639-705-7)

The Impasse by Franci McMahon. A horse-packing excursion into the Montana Wilderness becomes an adventure of terrifying proportions for Miles and ten women on an outfitter-led trip. (978-1-62639-781-1)

The Right Kind of Wrong by PJ Trebelhorn. Bartender Quinn Burke is happy with her life as a playgirl until she realizes she can't fight her feelings any longer for her best friend, bookstore owner Grace Everett. (978-1-62639-771-2)

Wishing on a Dream by Julie Cannon. Can two women change everything for the chance at love? (978-1-62639-762-0)

A Quiet Death by Cari Hunter. When the body of a young Pakistani girl is found out on the moors, the investigation leaves Detective Sanne Jensen facing an ordeal she may not survive. (978-1-62639-815-3)

Buried Heart by Laydin Michaels. When Drew Chambliss meets Cicely Jones, her buried past finds its way to the surface. Will they survive its discovery or will their chance at love turn to dust? (978-1-62639-801-6)

Escape: Exodus Book Three by Gun Brooke. Aboard the Exodus ship *Pathfinder*, President Thea Tylio still holds Caya Lindemay, a clairvoyant changer, in protective custody, which has devastating consequences endangering their relationship and the entire Exodus mission. (978-1-62639-635-7)

Genuine Gold by Ann Aptaker. New York, 1952. Outlaw Cantor Gold is thrown back into her honky-tonk Coney Island past, where crime and passion simmer in a neon glare. (978-1-62639-730-9)

Into Thin Air by Jeannie Levig. When her girlfriend disappears, Hannah Lewis discovers her world isn't as orderly as she thought it was. (978-1-62639-722-4)

Night Voice by CF Frizzell. When talk show host Sable finally acknowledges her risqué radio relationship with a mysterious caller, she welcomes a *real* relationship with local tradeswoman Riley Burke. (978-1-62639-813-9)

Raging at the Stars by Lesley Davis. When the unbelievable theories start revealing themselves as truths, can you trust in the ones who have conspired against you from the start? (978-1-62639-720-0)

She Wolf by Sheri Lewis Wohl. When the hunter becomes the hunted, more than love might be lost. (978-1-62639-741-5)

Smothered and Covered by Missouri Vaun. The last person Nash Wiley expects to bump into over a two a.m. breakfast at Waffle House is her college crush, decked out in a curve-hugging law enforcement uniform. (978-1-62639-704-0)

The Butterfly Whisperer by Lisa Moreau. Reunited after ten years, can Jordan and Sophie heal the past and rediscover love or will differing desires keep them apart? (978-1-62639-791-0)